CHIMNEY POND TALES
Yarns told by LeRoy Dudley

PAMOLA
PEAK *

CHIMNEY
PEAK *

INDEX
ROCK

THE KNIFE EDGE

CART TRACKS

TO
PAMOLA'S CAVE

This Is Where the Stories Happened

* Asterisks mark the location of three peaks which – when viewed from Chimney Pond – are hidden by buttresses .

The mountain is actually wrapped around the pond as indicated by the words, East, South, and West. See *Pamola's World* at the back of the book.

WEST

SOUTH
PEAK*

BAXTER
PEAK

THE
CATHEDRALS

THE   SADDLE
SADDLE
SLIDE

DUDLEY'S DEN

Jane

PAMOLA talking with
his friend and advisor ɔOY DUDLEY
As described t. MAURICE DAY
AUG. 1933

CHIMNEY POND TALES

YARNS TOLD BY
LEROY DUDLEY

Assembled by

CLAYTON HALL and JANE THOMAS

with

ELIZABETH HALL HARMON

Illustrated by Jane Thomas

ISBN -10   0-9631718-0-1
ISBN-13   0-978-9631718-0-1

Published by
The Pamola Press, 11 Blackstrap Road,
Cumberland, Maine 04021

First Printing December, 1991
Second Printing, June, 1992
Third Printing May, 1994
Fourth Printing December 1997
Fifth Printing July 2006

Table of Contents

List of Illustrations

ACKNOWLEDGMENTS

There are many people whom we must acknowledge for their help and support as this book has evolved. First and foremost must be the late Clayton Hall, who, in the early thirties, back-packed an Edison office dictating machine seven miles in to Chimney Pond from Windey Pitch, recorded Roy's tales on wax cylinders, and laboriously transcribed them to produce his first draft. It was a labor of love, to be sure.

We also must express our gratitude to the late Maurice "Jake" Day, who was to have illustrated Clayton Hall's book and who checked out my drawings of Pamola and pronounced them fit. Our visit with him felt like a special gift.

To Jon Hall, who made it possible for us to hear *Pamola's Last Lady Friend* on the original cylinder, go our heartfelt thanks. Without his help, Beth would never have heard Roy's voice, and we would never have known Arvesta Pelateekahawn.

To Jonathan Thomas, to Russell Harmon of the next generation, and to Ira Hartman go special thanks for their valuable time and technical assistance with their computers.

Many others who have cheered us on are mentioned in *Listening to Roy*. We've had real impetus from people at Baxter Park, both the staff and the Advisory, from our friends and relations, from our families, and from each other to keep going till it's done. Thanks go to all.

Jane Thomas and Beth Harmon
July, 1991

THE STORYTELLER

These are the tales of Mark Leroy Dudley of Mount Katahdin, who guided there from the 1890's until his death in 1942. During those years he became nationally famous among mountaineers and outdoorsmen for his tall tales about Pamola, the God of Thunder and Protector of the mountain, as well as other stories of his life in the North Woods of Maine.

Roy was born June 4, 1873, in Wesley, Maine. He was the fourth of eleven children, the oldest son. The family apparently moved to Princeton when Roy was a baby and to Stacyville when he was five or six years old, so Roy grew up in the shadow of Mt. Katahdin. His father, Mark Dudley, was a woodsman, and undoubtedly hustled for a living at this and that, as lots of folks did in those days and still do in eastern Maine. People lived by any combination of farming, trapping, logging, handcrafts and general skulduggery that would put food on the table, clothes on their backs and a roof overhead. Life was hard. Pleasures and entertainments were home-made and often very good indeed.

Roy's dad could well remember his own father's long-time friendship with Governor John Neptune, of the Penobscot Indian tribe. Neptune was a well-known fur trapper whose winter range covered a wide area of northern and eastern Maine. He was known as a shaman, that is a person possessing magical powers, and was said to have defeated a great loathsome monster in hand to hand combat. People claimed Neptune could throw his voice for miles. He was also legendary as a lady's man, responsible for a serious political rift within the tribe, but that's another story.

Neptune may have been related to Roy's grand-dad. There's some tradition that Roy had Indian blood. Certainly, if Roy's tales are any testimony, there was a good deal of shamanistic lore afloat in the Dudley family. He had an Indian style of telling a story, with much detail and scene-setting as well as some of the eastern Algonquin dark humor, which still lurks in Down-East gossip and tale-telling.

xi

At any rate, as Roy was growing up his dad filled him full of stories, many about Pamola and Katahdin. He told one tale about how Neptune had outfoxed Pamola and survived a winter night on the mountain. "Old Governor" said he had gone to the mountain, in the wintertime, against all warnings, and had camped overnight in a small cabin, somewhere close to the mountain. During the night he said that Pamola had tugged and pounded and raged at the door, trying to get at him, but the door was frozen shut so Pamola could not reach his prey. I suspect Old Governor poured water under the door himself to freeze it shut. At dawn Pamola flew away in disgust and Neptune made fast tracks out of there. That was Neptune's story, as Roy's family told it.

So with this background Roy grew up eager to explore the mountain and meet Pamola himself. At about the age of fourteen he went to work as a cook in a lumber camp somewhere near the mountain. In time he grew fonder of the mountain than he was of lumbering and he guided his first scientist on the mountain at the age of eighteen. This was James H. Emerton of Salem, Massachusetts, a well-known entomologist and scientific illustrator specializing in spiders. Emerton is immortalized by Roy in story as well as in his own numerous scientific publications.

For much of his life Roy spent his summers guiding and his winters trapping and probably turned a hand to many things. He was a game warden for many years, and the Maine Fish and Game Department did well to hire him. The saying goes, "It takes one to catch one." He was married twice and left four children.

Roy guided mainly north and east of Katahdin and into the Great Basin of the mountain, camping at Chimney Pond. Before automobiles, he would meet clients at the railroad in Stacyville, traveling by wagon to a place called Happy Corner. From there it was a two-day trip by buckboard or on foot to Katahdin Lake, stopping overnight at Lunksoos Camp on the East Branch of the Penobscot River. Parties walked from Katahdin Lake to Chimney Pond, with pack horses carrying the heaviest gear such as tents, blankets, camp tools and food. Governor Percival Baxter, the founder and creator of Baxter Park, visited Katahdin this way in 1922 with a group of about a dozen other men.

By himself or with only one "sport", Roy could camp under the sheltering rock on the southwest side of Chimney Pond, but the space was limited and the blackflies pestiferous on that side of the pond, so for larger parties he packed in tents. In 1917 he built a leanto which was called Dudley's Den and which remained standing and in use until somtime in the late forties. A temporary cabin was erected for a scientific party about 1900, but it was only usable for one season. The first permanent cabin was built by Roy and a helper for the Maine Fish and Game Department in 1924. This cabin was replaced by the Baxter Park Authority in the late sixties.

Over the years Roy guided a great number of scientists, artists, and famous personalities besides Governor Baxter. Some were there to study the mountain and its flora and fauna; others were there simply to enjoy it. Many of these men and women maintained a lifelong love and respect for Roy. His hospitality, kindness, knowledge and common sense, along with his wondrous tales and sense of humor, endeared him to these visitors. Roy in turn became a rather knowledgeable botanist as a result of his association with the naturalists. The interaction was fruitful to all parties. Many famous men and women were proud to be his friends.

On the other hand, let some "Great Man" act superior and talk down to his guide, then the man of the mountain could turn to stone. There were a few of these great ones who "blew" their chance to become acquainted with a real giant. There are always men too small to recognize true greatness.

Roy was truly great; no doubt about that. Like many Maine people, he was not much limited by his geographic restraints. He traveled little in body, but ranged far in his thinking, his reading and his friendships. A true literary person with broad perspective, active imagination, and great humor can hardly be held down just by living in one place all his life.

Roy wrote stories in his mind, and told them: a disappearing literary form. His tales were based on his cultural heritage, his kindly regard for human frailty, and his own experience of the world around him. To print them removes them from their true mode, but memory storytelling goes in and out of fashion. To record them will preserve them.

You wouldn't find a kinder man than Roy. In the backwoods tradition he had the cardinal virtue: "He'd take the shirt off his back to help someone." He always had a pot of tea on to brew, often an old saucepan or the top of an old blue double-boiler. He'd start her up in the morning by throwing a handful of tea-leaves into a pan of cold water and setting it on the woodstove. As the day wore on he might add water or tea-leaves, or subtract tea as he felt it appropriate. By evening, if anyone showed up cold and tired he had the sovereign remedy. Many said you could pour out a yard of that tea and stand it up in the corner. After drinking a cupful you could lick your weight in wildcats. Some warned us not to pour Roy's tea into an aluminum cup since it was apt to eat through the bottom of the cup before you'd have time to drink it. That tea was hard on our tooth enamel, but I don't doubt it saved many a life and quite a few marriages.

Roy made you feel welcome, warm, and loved. If you were cold and wet, he'd be sure to dry you out and might insist you stay in the cabin just that first night. He'd mother-hen a whole campground full of people without seeming to, and see that they had sound advice for their own safety before they "clim" the mountain. He sometimes gave someone his own bed and he and his wife slept over across the pond under the sheltering rock.

When Dudley died in February, 1942, he was mourned by friends and admirers all over the United States. *Appalachia*, the journal of the Appalachian Mountain Club, published an *in memoriam* note, most lovingly written by Mr. Ronald Gower, himself an authority on Katahdin and a frequent guest at Chimney Pond. Following the end of World War II, the club placed a bronze plaque in memory of Roy on a boulder near the state camp at Chimney Pond. The inscription reads in part, "He loved this mountain."   J.T.

CLAYTON HALL ON DUDLEY - 1937

Seven years ago I met Roy Dudley over a cup of tea at Chimney Pond. It was after ten miles of heavy packing and some two thousand feet of rocky trail. My companion, a seasoned guide, pointed out a singular thing: Here was a man in such perfect condition he could handle a ten-foot log as though it were a match-stick.

Two years later a party of ten sat down to supper at Chimney Pond Cabin. When we had done with our supper, a botanist lit his pipe and turned to Dudley for a story. The man leaned forward on the table. He began. Behold a real legend-teller! His narrative was quaint...and it was droll. Our company was rocked with gale on gale of laughter. The gentleman's humor was blunt and delicate by turns, the word pictures vivid and at times...poetry. He loved the music of little sounds: "good, good, good," water bubbled from the jug. He was at once a child in imagination and a man in his cool flow of language. He was very like an Indian. ...Such drolleries and mysteries haunted me. They should never be lost.

Spring, summer, fall and winter passed and passed again, but nothing came of my plans. Finally one winter I set out to find Dudley. It was one of the most breathtaking adventures of my life. For three days I traveled in the north woods...alone. I was determined to hunt and trap with the old man of the mountain and record such stories as he told me.

I went to live in a little log hut on the East Branch of the Penobscot River. Evenings by lamplight I toiled over a journal. The old trapper told many a saga of pioneers in these woods, but I did not again hear the legends of the mountain I longed to hear. When in March winds I bade him goodbye, he smiled as he alone can smile and said, "Come to the mountain in spring. It's beautiful; just like a garden!"

June happened along and with it a memorable letter: "Dear Friend: Am in hopes to see you soon. Roy Dudley."

It was at Chimney Pond that he told me the legends of Pamola. Let me tell you about that place. High in the mountain is the Great Basin. Within it Dudley has built his cabin home. Once seated on his porch you can take in the green vistas before you. There are spruces and below them the deep green of the pond. Far above and on every side rises the eternal rock. Let no writer...picture it. That I leave to the forest's grand old man who will not sicken you with "style", but catch its holy glory in simple words.

The old camp is the soul of the woodsman's craft. It is seldom that one sees better axe carpentry. Dudley, with the help of one man, cut and trimmed the fifty logs in a day. The simplicity and compactness of this little cabin cannot be exaggerated. Each log and roof pole is as neatly joined as if it had grown there. Precise craftsmanship is a joy to behold. Often I lay awake when the first rays of the sun crept into the camp. There in the early light I could study the roof structure.

When the wind whistles around the cabin the old man will always light up his pipe... "Well, you know the old camp never would stand thet wind if I hadn't spiked her through!" Then he tells how he argued it over with Alex Mullin. "I saw he was using six-inch spikes and I says, 'Them'll never hold the camp here!' He asked me what was the idea of all the spiking. I told him he'd see if it come a good gale!"

This is without doubt the most homey little cabin in the world. Percy Baxter, who bought this mountain and gave it to the State of Maine, still insists that it's "Roy's mountain". His portrait presides over the rude dining table.... "To Roy Dudley of Mt. Katahdin from his companion and friend."

Here is a friendly place. From far off you scent woodsmoke and a supper cooking. Then lamplight glows in a window. Once within, the camp is yours. Though Abby Dudley[1] is not living, her charm stays. Upon the windows are her curtains. The shelves are lined with her blue plaid. Upon the wall hangs her bread board and rolling pin. In the corner, under the lamp-bracket, is the little stove. That stove came up on the back of the old man of the mountain. He sometimes joked about having packed loads that "would puzzle a horse to carry."

---

1. Roy's second wife, Abby, died November 8, 1934, according to Stacyville town records. She was given an obituary in APPALACHIA, Vol. XX, No. 79-80, Winter, 1935, p. 419.

What are very characteristic of Mr. Dudley are his pipe, his cup of tea, and his pungent observations. I might say, while sitting on the cabin porch, "Roy, have you seen those Dartmouth boys up there today?" ...A quick removal of the pipe and a squint of the eyes... "No, and if I could, they'd look like a fly turd on a map of the world!"

Dudley deals in an epic hero. Pamola is a familiar Indian spirit. A person could hardly live sixty winters near Katahdin without coming under Pamola's spell.

Roy Dudley shows Indian features in his face and in his manner of speech and thought. I have often heard him speak of "the Indian in me." I accept this as evidence that his is part Indian blood. ...Ask Dudley where the mink lives: "That gentleman lives in under banks, in old logs, and in old muskrat dens." There is something in the timbre of his voice that tells you he speaks as readily of mink as of the Smiths or Joneses.

While it is the obvious thing to say that he knows the forest, I have been struck with the thought that the forest knows him! There's a thing sublime in seeing the old trapper off in the distance swallowed up in an eddying snow squall. He wanders in and out among bleak stubbs far away on the swamp's edge. Nature wraps him gently 'round with her blanket of snow and spruces.

LISTENING TO ROY

My brother and I grew up here in Maine. Our childhood was blessed with storytellers, but of all the beloved men who set us to giggling with their wry tales, Roy Dudley of Mount Katahdin was the star. Our world turned around Roy for the few enchanted summers we knew him. My family made numerous stays at his camps at Chimney Pond, in the very heart of the mountain. From there we explored the rest of the mountain and also just lived there as neighbors of Roy, his housekeeper, Sue, his old friend Pop Kimball and others. I was eight the first summer I went along. I played, explored by myself, called on other climbers, who were few in those days, and visited Roy and Sue. Mother said any time she couldn't find me I would turn up in Roy's cabin listening to him yarn.

What a spinner he was! Obviously fond of children, he responded to our simplest comments and questions with stories, as you will see. The summer of 1940 Roy wasn't feeling too well and for most of two weeks I camped on a footstool by his bedside every day till Sue drove me off so he could get some rest.

What I particularly remember of Roy's storytelling was his matter-of-factness. He never really dropped the story-line at any time, at least not with us kids, and I think not much with grown folks either. The stories weren't hauled out as stories only, they were his history. He alluded to their events in normal conversation as naturally as he'd mention yesterday's chores. He certainly did tell stories in the usual way, but he'd also mention something his friend Pamola did or said just in passing, as he'd mention anyone else he knew.

Showing me Jake Day's delightful drawing of himself and Pamola he said, "Mr. Day took this picture of us when he was up here working for Mr. Disney. He had us set up there on Pamola Peak and he stood over on Chimley Peak to take the picture. Haint thet a good likeness?" You never knew where storytelling began and conversation left off. I find it's still my natural way to explain Roy's tales to folks: Mount Katahdin is inhabited by a demon named Pamola who used to keep people out of the mountain. When Dudley first went there he made friends with the old fellow, and many of his stories are about their adventures while getting acquainted. Of course there are also stories about other folks.

One story that arose naturally and came naturally into many a conversation was Fifteen Fry Pans. Up over the door and windows on the front wall inside the kitchen of the State camp, hanging on a row of nails driven into the logs, was a great long row of frying pans, the old "tin" ones, with the hollow handles. There were two or three big ones and a whole string of six-inchers. It was quite a display. Naturally anyone coming in there for the first time would say, "Where in the world did all those fry pans come from?"

The answer had variants. When I asked him, he said, "One day, back a few years, seemed's tho' it was early in October, we was getting ready to move back to Stacyville for the winter. I was down to the shore of the pond, there, scrubbing out my two fry pans with sand when my wife called to ask me something or other so I left what I was doing and went to help her. Anyways, we got all packed up and headed on down the trail and we was clean to Basin Pond before I remembered the fry pans! Well, I was kind of disgusted but I says, 'I haint going back just for them old tin pans when I can get another one for thirty-five cents!' So the pans stayed right there all winter.

"Well, sir, next spring when we come back here in May, I went down to the pond for a bucket of water. When I got to the edge of the pond I looked and Lo and Behold, those two fry pans had spawned! There they was, with their little ones all around 'em, jest as nice as could be. So I gathered 'em all up and brought 'em up to the camp and there you see 'em on the wall."

Well, I thought that was pretty interesting, so come suppertime, I told my family about it. Right away my brother Herb spoke up, "Gee, that IS interesting. Last summer I asked Roy the same question and he told it another way. He said one spring he was in here by himself and he got pretty lonesome so he caught himself a pretty little partridge to keep as a pet. He didn't have anything to make a pen for her, so he tied a fry pan to her leg to keep her from running away. He said he had her about a week when one day she didn't come to his call and after a few more days he figured a martin had eaten her. Then after about three more weeks, she showed up one morning with a whole brood of chicks. She still had the fry pan tied to her leg and each little chicky had a little fry pan tied to its leg. So he untied all the fry pans and there they are!"

As you will see, he told it yet another way, another time!

Often folks would ask for stories and Roy would oblige them. Sometimes a group just happened to be together, either on the front porch or in the cabin, or sometimes he would entertain a large party at the big group leanto that stood up behind the cabin a way, where he would stand by the fire and recount his history with occasional gestures, pointing out a location on the mountain, or augmenting his description. I can still see him turning his hand up to demonstrate "a mean little piece of birch bark no bigger than your hand" as he told the pipe story. Like many storytellers he would partly act his characters, striking postures and modifying his voice to suit the person speaking.

And always a perfectly straight face! (How I envy that!) His eyes would twinkle like all the stars in the sky, fairly snap, at the most outrageous bits, but he'd never lose composure. His timing was flawless. No second punch line of Roy's ever was lost in previous laughter. He was far too savvy for that.

The stories stuck. Herb and I were obsessed with them, told them, and remembered them ever after. However, for many years I believed that nobody but my own family wanted to hear them. Then in July 1978 I hesitatingly invited John Gordon, who was then the ranger at Chimney Pond, to sit in while I retold some of the tales to my family. He and others at Baxter Park urged me on to see that the stories were recorded, since we thought that there was no written record of them left.

Now I had heard, back in 1939, that someone had written

down Roy's tales and was preparing a book, but that the writer, a Mr. Clayton Hall of Milo, had been taken ill and publication was held up. That book never happened, Roy died, war came, people scattered and all these forty years later, I believed the manuscript must have been lost, since no one at Baxter Park seemed aware of its ever having existed. So I went ahead on my own.

Then a miracle occurred. About a third of the way into the project, the old manuscript surfaced in the hands of Beth Harmon of Cumberland, an heir of Clayton Hall. Beth contacted Baxter Park headquarters, looking for "someone who knew Dudley". Buzz Caverly and Gerald Merry both referred her letter to me and a most enjoyable collaboration has resulted. Beth had material I'd been wishing for, like the porcupine story, which I think I heard but couldn't remember, and more stories that I was unaware of, especially more about Pamola's family life. I, in turn had one story that had evolved after the Hall manuscript was put together. Best of all we seemed to see eye to eye on what to do with all of it. The project has been a pleasure.

The Indians of Maine believed that Katahdin was inhabited by at least two spirits, one the noble spirit of the mountain and the other the demon, Pamola, whose mission was to keep people away from the high slopes. Early Indian tales tell of two young women who respond to the mountain-as-man. One is gathering blueberries near the mountain and says, "If Katahdin were a man, I'd marry him." The other, expressing her firm intent to remain single, says, "I'll never marry! Even if Katahdin turned into a man, I wouldn't even marry him!" The former becomes the devoted wife of the good spirit, Katahdin; the latter the shrewish harridan wife of Pamola, the ugly thunder-demon. (Pamola should have thought twice!)

Mount Katahdin has a unique personality. Mountains do, but as with people, you have to see and meet Katahdin to understand what he is like. Since I first met Katahdin, it has seemed easy to say, "Oh, mountain, I love you! If you were a man I'd sure marry you if you'd have me." My feelings may be influenced by the spirit of my Indian ever-so-great grandmother.

It might seem odd that someone with real respect for the Indian traditions would seem to be promulgating something like an outrageous spoof on the originals. In fact these tales are not a spoof at all. The Indian tales themselves contained much of the outrageous, the fearsome and the brutal as well as the marvelous and the inspiring. If you've grown up on Hiawatha, go read some real Algonquin legends and you'll see what I mean. Much is wonderful; all is sacred; yet in a certain sense nothing is sacred. (For instance there is the Cree legend of the First Fart.)[2]

There are many elements: Pamola's traditional personality, a loving irreverence, and particular story details that seem to come straight from Indian tradition into Roy Dudley's tales. His way of telling tales showed this kinship, too. Compared with familiar European folk tales, these stories are heavy with scene setting and corroborative detail. I found myself checking almanacs and old records, just to verify details, which makes no objective sense whatever. However, that's the way Roy's storytelling affected me. I lost the line between story and history, which was exactly Roy's intent. Never mind! That's fine with me! I see Dudley's experiences with Pamola as no more than what you'd expect might have happened, given the personalities and the terrain involved.

This book got started because of friends and family, and it couldn't have happened without their help and support. It was finished in this far more complete form because of the total ease with which I have been able to work with my collaborator, Beth and her family. The project has brought about new friendships as well as a new book.

My dear old brother, Herb, who died while the first draft was in preparation, also played an important role in preserving the tales. It was he who remembered the tale about the Widow Woman from Portland, which would otherwise have been lost.

---

2. Bauer, George W., CREE TALES AND BELIEFS, Northeast Folklore Society, Vol. XII, Orono, Maine, 1971.

Whenever these stories are read or told, we two will still sit together in spirit, on the floor of a log camp at Chimney Pond, hugging our knees and yelling with laughter at Roy.

You'll really get acquainted with Roy through reading his tales. But for starters, picture in your mind a lithe, well-knit man, not very tall, slowed by years, but still active. He comes up the path from the pond carrying a pail of water, more slowly this year, but still walking like a bobcat. He smiles and sets down his bucket. "Well, there's Jenny!" He kisses Jenny. "You made good time!" A handshake for the boys. "There you are, darlin! You're lookin lovely!" A kiss for Jenny's mom. "Wunt you come in for a cup a tea? I cut boughs for your bed this morning. You can fix it yourselves. You'll have Number One Pamola Avenue. I drove the Boy Scouts out of it this morning." (The boys were leaving anyway.) His welcome mat was velvet!

One morning in February, when we were just beginning to think about another grand week at Chimney Pond in July, Dad looked at the morning paper and said, "Good Lord, Roy's been killed!" We all read the newspaper in grim disbelief. Roy had slipped on the ice and fallen under a logging truck. Our consolation was that he had died while still active. He was on his way to check his fur traps when the accident occurred. He died with his boots on in any case.

It was war-time. Gasoline was rationed and none of our group could attend a distant funeral. We sent telegrams to friends out of state, and each of us mourned in his own way. We still do.

J.T.

ROY DUDLEY: SELF-PORTRAIT

I was born in the year of eighteen and seventy-four. My father's name was Mark Dudley. Father was a veteran of the Civil War. We ought to tell what he did after the war. He was what they called a shingle-weaver in those days — shaved cedar shingles. I can remember when I was a little feller, sitting on a log and watching him pull off the big shavings. I couldn't have been more than four years old and I can remember how nice the cedar wood used to smell. New cedar! It did, too!

If people in those days had what the poorest have now they'd think themselves lucky. I've known families and families who had no floor in their cabins — nothing but the bare ground. Yes, in those days people were awful hard put. I can remember when Mother used to go around and divide the bread amongst us — a junk to each one with a piece of deer meat. Many's the night I've gone to bed without my supper.

Father, he was always trapping and guiding, so I guess that's where I took it from, as I was always in the woods when I was a small boy. I knew the woods and forest at that time as well as any man. I knew where all the game hung out and all the fish in the lakes and streams. Father allowed me to carry a gun as soon as I was big enough to shoulder one. The first party I guided was to the old Mountain. First I started carrying packs on my back and next was with a pack horse. My headquarters was at Chimney Pond.

The pond is located in the South Basin of Mt. Katahdin. It's a small body of clear silvery water, about eight acres in size, surrounded by walls of granite reaching into the sky. The South Basin is like a huge bowl with the side facing the northeast broken out. The sides of the bowl are granite ledges two thousand feet in height. Chimney Pond, with its clear waters, forms the bottom of the bowl. The cabin itself is twenty-nine hundred and thirteen feet up and is located on the northeast side of the pond. On the

1

west side is Cathedral Rock with its spears reaching high up into the sky. At the east end of the ledge, about five hundred feet up and about the same distance down around the shoulder, there, the traveler can see a dark hole where Pamola makes his abode. On moonlight nights he comes out and flops them great wings and flies around over the basin.

In all there's ten peaks on the mountain: Pamola, Chimney, South, Baxter, Hamlin, and the four peaks called Howe Peaks and the Northwest Peak.

That explains the mountain except the heights of it and the Zane Gray stuff; he spends time describing out the colors. I think when the mountain looks prettiest is about the twentieth of June when everything is coming to life after its long winter sleep. The top of the mountain at that time is dotted with patches of Diapensia in bloom that resemble patches of snow. And around the rocks is the Rhododendron Pink sticking out and patches of Dwarf Laurel with its cup-shaped blossoms. There's places around the ledges where Lazalia[3] grows with its fine leaves and its pink blossoms mixed in with the Cassiope[4] with its pearlish white. It seems as though there's life in everything at that time of the year.

Down around the cabin early in the morning you can hear the song of the hermit thrush as he hops along the little brook that runs through the yard; also the white-throated sparrow with his sweet song which I love so well. And there's other birds: the purple finch, the crossbill, the rock wren, the flycatcher, and junco. In the evening the little rabbits are hopping around the yard to get the green grass that grows. The marten are quite plentiful and oh, what thieves!

We won't say anything about the blackflies. They rise from every bush in swarms and blind you, crawl in your collar and in every button hole. They come to keep you from being lonesome.

---

3. Alpine Azalea (*Loiseleuria procumbens*)
4. Also called Moss Plant (*Cassiope hyphoides*)

THE RAFT OF CROWBARS

When I was a small boy, you see, about seven years old, Father used to tell me tales of Pamola and how he'd destroy the Indians. One time he said an old Indian by the name of John Neptune had stayed at the house and told him a lot about Pamola.

The years didn't seem to go fast enough for me to grow up so I could get to the mountain and see for myself. I kept Pamola on my mind continually. When I was about fifteen years old I went to Katahdin. I cruised two or three days around the rocks and ledges and looked in all the dark holes under rocks, in hopes to see Pamola. I failed to see him but I liked the old mountain.

So time passed and I became a guide taking parties onto the mountain, and that's the way I earned my living.

One day I had taken a party out. They went down the west side of the mountain to take their canoes and go down the West Branch. I returned to Chimney Pond and made ready to camp alone. This was August and the moon was at its full. I lay down but I couldn't go to sleep as it was awful hot that night. I kept turning and twisting on the balsam bed, and at last I got up and went down to the shore of the pond where I could get a cool breeze. It was somewhere around quarter of twelve when I lay down and kind of dozed off. All of a sudden I was awakened by a splashing in the water. Lo and behold, there was Pamola on a raft paddling around the pond!

It seemed as though the raft was made of large crowbars[5] and the longer he paddled, the faster she went. I sat there trembling and looking. He was the ugliest looking critter I ever saw in my

---

5. Raft of Crowbars: Tradition has it that in the Algonquin belief system the ability to make iron or stone float on water was sure proof that one had magical powers.

3

life. I knew he had to be Pamola. He stood up about eighteen or twenty feet tall, with body and legs like a man, but all covered with coarse hair like a moose. His head was like a moose and his ears and horns, but he had kind of a big curved beak like an eagle. He had a great long beard on his chin, as much as three feet long or longer. It was parted in the wind, there, with the ends blowing back over his shoulders as he paddled along.

He had the queerest feet you ever saw. They had three great pointed toes like a chicken, and one that pointed backwards. He had big wings growing out of his shoulders, but just like a bat's wings. He was a fierce looking sight! I lay still in the bushes; dassn't move.

Finally it seemed as though he'd sailed enough. He took his raft, flew up on the side of the mountain, and hid it back of some ledges. I looked at my watch and it was just one o'clock exactly. I didn't see him any more for a while. I was sitting there thinking what an awful looking man he was. I was satisfied in my mind that I had seen Pamola, and it pleased me greatly. I have seen him many times since, but I have never got the same thrill.

At last the big full moon was striking the Knife Edge and I spied a dark shadow behind it. The moon rolled along over the boulders and this dark object followed it till it got to where the mountain slopes off the other way. That was the South Peak. I could plainly see then that it was Pamola rolling the moon over the Knife Edge!

He straightened up, flopped his great wings, let a hoot out of him like a loon and flew back into a dark hole in the mountain. Now I've found out since that he comes down and has his sail on the raft every month, the night the moon fulls.

5

MY FIRST ENCOUNTER WITH PAMOLA

This is the first time I ever talked with Pamola. It was the day after I first saw him paddling his raft and rolling the moon across the Knife Edge. That very next morning a group of folks came in looking to climb the mountain. They asked me if I'd show them the best way up to the top. They were an adventuresome group of two young ministers and their girl friends. They wanted to climb to the top and then go down the other side to meet their guides at Abol on the West Branch. Well, I'd figured out a good way to get up the side of Pamola Peak so I guided them over the mountain to the old Abol Trail. Then I decided to walk down to Abol with them and see if I could trade with their guides for some pipe tobacco. I got back to Chimney Pond just about nightfall.

Now this was a lively group of young folks and it seemed as though all their giggling and hollering and singing and yodeling and whatnot had attracted Pamola's attention so as he realized for the first time there was someone around. I was back to camp and I had had my supper. So I was sitting in the shelter with the tea kettle still on the fire. After supper I had piled some big spruce logs about three foot long and a foot through onto the fire, lit my pipe, laid back on the balsam boughs, enjoying a smoke, and I was watching the sparks go up off the wood, with their tails disappearing in the air.

All at once I heard a noise which sounded between the rumble of thunder and the drum of a partridge. It seemed to come from up on the side of Pamola Peak, right on the skyline, there. Then I could see two big lights; looked like the headlights of a Model T Ford shining right at me. I could feel the hair on the back of my neck commence to rise up as those two lights started coming right towards me through the air. They kept drawing closer and I kept my eyes right on them till they lit right in front of the fire. There stood old Pamola! And when he folded them huge wings, the wind of them drove those logs rolling across the yard. Sparks and smoke and cinders flew!

Now I was some scared but I knew I'd ought not to show it with a feller like Pamola. So I says, "Welcome, Friend. Won't you have a cup of tea?"

Pamola, he grabbed the tea kettle off the fire and swallowed the whole potful at a gulp, boiling hot. Then he began to rave. "THIS IS ALL MINE! THIS IS ALL MINE!"

I was so frightened I crawled just as far back into the shelter as I could get. Then I mustered what courage I had left and said, "What's all yours?"

He waved his hand all around, taking in the whole mountain. "THIS," he says, "IS ALL MINE! THIS IS MY MOUNTAIN. GO AWAY!"

I took a minute to pull my courage together a little more and I says, "But I like it here. I mean to stay."

"NOBODY STAYS HERE BUT ME! THIS IS MINE! YOU SHALL NEVER REMAIN HERE IN PEACE!"

"Well," I says, "I mean to stay, all the same."

Then Pamola pointed a long finger at me and screamed, "YOU! YOU WILL REGRET IT! I'VE WARNED YOU!" and he flapped his big wings, sending sparks flying all over the clearing, and flew off, roaring and screaming, to his cave.

As soon as he was out of sight I could hear a drumming sound coming from over to the cave. Big heavy clouds started rolling in, shutting out the moon and stars. Then the rain came and the thunder came and the lightning came. The wind howled and roared! It sounded like an express train coming over the rocks. Trees fell, torn up by the roots. It was the dreadfullest thunder storm I'd ever seen before that time, though I saw some worse after that. I was getting wet and I was pretty scared but I knew from the old Indian stories that that was half of Pamola's magic: to scare you good. So I gritted my teeth and stuck it out till morning. It was little sleep I got that night.

Daylight finally come and the storm let up. You should have seen the mess! All my bedding and clothing was wet and most of my food was soaked and spoiled. But I wasn't going to give in. I hid my salt pork and my matches, spread things out in the sun to dry and hiked down to Basin Pond to catch some fish so as I wouldn't go hungry.

That afternoon I came back to find all my fireplace rocks piled in under the shelter so I couldn't get in. My clothes and blankets and kettles were scattered all over five acres. I gathered up what I could find, hauled most of the rocks out so as I'd have some room to sleep, and re-built my fireplace. Then I cooked my fish, ate my supper and rolled up in my blankets for the night.

Pretty soon I commenced to hear thunder and before you knew it there was another storm going, worse than the night before. The wind blew something fierce. Big trees went pitch-poling across the basin. It was ferocious! But I stayed right there. Next morning I hid everything well and went to Basin Pond again for fish.

The third night the same thing happened. The storm got so bad that there was two or three new rock slides came down the headwall. Mighty boulders as big as houses were bouncing around the basin like basketballs. Still I didn't budge. After that there were a few more half-hearted storms but I guess I was stubborner than Old Pamola. Anyways he seemed to peter out on the game after a while, and I stayed.

THE WIDOW-WOMAN FROM PORTLAND

With all those thunderstorms it didn't take a college professor to see that old Pamola was trying to drive me out of here, but after he give up it seemed as though he was just trying to ignore me. After things had settled down a mite, I decided I could build me a camp, so I went out a couple days to get spikes and roofing nails and tar paper to build me a shelter over on this side of the pond where the blackflies ain't so bad.

I fixed up a nice log leanto with a bough bed on poles up off the ground and a good rock fireplace, and by that time my first month was up. It was time to head out to Katahdin Lake to meet a party I'd promised to guide in here. It was this widow-woman from Portland. She was pretty well-off I suppose. Anyway I'd been taking her trout fishing, spring and fall, for a couple of years.

I'd seen her earlier that spring and I made the worst blunder! I made mention I was coming in here to explore and she was all for coming right along, first trip. Well, I didn't plan for that because she was such a talker. I thought two weeks would be more than a man could stand. So I says, "No, it might be danger-ous."

"Oh," she says, "that's no matter. I love danger. It'll make the trip more exciting."

I says, "There wunt be any shelter except maybe a big rock or a spruce tree."

She says, "But you could carry in a tent." And that's the way the talk went for about three hours and a half! Finally I persuad-ed her to wait till I'd had a month to look things over and she'd persuaded me, against better judgment, to come out in a month to tell her all about it, she said. But it was obvious she'd be at Katahdin Lake with all her gear for a trip and I was resigned to it. Anyways, now it was time so I headed for Katahdin Lake.

I got to the lake early. It was a beautiful morning, peaceful and quiet. There wasn't a sign of the widow woman. I knew she'd be along pretty soon, so I just sat back enjoying the silence, watching the little cat's-paws of breezes playing on the pond and listening to the white-throated sparrow just singing his head off over along the shore.

Then, right on time, about five minutes to ten, I started hearing this steady talking noise coming along the trail, so I knew she was coming. Sure enough, about seven minutes later out of the woods she came with a man and a horse she'd hired to bring her gear in from Happy Corner.[6] The man and the horse both looked like someone had been pounding them on the head. I guess it was all the words they'd had hitting them all morning, because they both looked relieved, once she turned the stream of words toward me and we got headed for Chimney Pond.

Of course when we got here to Chimney Pond, there was lots more for her to talk about. There were the trees, the cliffs, the water, the sky, the flowers, and on and on. It seemed as though she never had a bit of trouble thinking of things to talk about, and that made things easy for me. I didn't have any trouble not listening to her most of the time, so her and me got along just fine!

She had a grand time. She loved the old mountain, and we clim it this way and that. We picked a way over to the North Basin. We clim Hamlin Ridge and the Cathedrals and covered most of the mountain, altogether. She said she just adored all the lovely views and the gorgeous scenery, and she said a whole lot more I really didn't hear.

Then one morning at breakfast I made a mistake and mentioned about Pamola. I never should have done that. As soon as she heard of Pamola nothing in the world would do till she met him. Now I didn't want any part of that at all, me not being on awful good terms with him myself. I just didn't know what

---

6. Happy Corner is in the town of Patten. In the early twenties this was where you changed from automobile to buckboard on the route from Patten to Lunksoos Camp on the East Branch. The route from there was by trail to Katahdin Lake, thence into the South Basin by way of Avalanche Field, roughly following what are now the Roaring Brook Road and the Chimney Pond Trail.

might happen, so I said, "Absolutely no! Out of the question!"

Well she begged and she pleaded for about three quarters of an hour and then she insisted and commanded and finally she wept and I couldn't stand it any longer, so reluctantly I gave in. We clim up to the caves where I thought Pamola made his camp, and when we got to the mouth of the first big cave I called out, "Hey, Pamola! There's someone here wants to meet you!"

Pamola come out of his cave and she starts right in, "Oh-Mr.-Pamola-I'm-so-delighted-to-meet-you-Mr.-Dudley-has-told-me-so-much-about-you-..." and on and on she went! I suddenly remembered that I had urgent business to take care of somewheres else and I made tracks for camp. But nothing much happened except that that woman talked and talked and talked and TALKED! Old Pamola was dumfoundered. He'd never seen anything like her in all his life. He couldn't get a word in cornerwise himself and he didn't know what to do with a critter like that.

Night came and the widow woman was still talking. Poor old Pamola couldn't get a bit of sleep. That woman just had so much she wanted to tell him! He tossed and turned on his bed in the cave but that infernal noise would not quit. Morning came and she was still going on at a great rate and Pamola's ears were starting to ring. To try to escape the awful din, he flew over to the Saddle and sat on the edge of the tableland with his feet down in the slide. That didn't bother the widow woman a bit; she just raised her voice a mite and kept right on talking.

About three days of that and I began to worry over Pamola's health. The poor old feller was getting dreadful tired and haggard from lack of sleep. It looked kind of like the shell shock to me. So I clim back up to the cave and more or less dragged the widow woman out of there bodily, got her down to camp, packed her up and headed out. I'd promised her a day fishing on Katahdin Lake and it was time to go anyways.

When we got to Katahdin Lake it was a nice warm day and there wasn't a bit of wind. I got my canoe out of the bushes and paddled us around so the widow-woman could fish and she had a fine time. The water was just as calm as could be — not a ripple

13

on the lake. It was as smooth as glass. I never saw such a lovely day and the fish were biting, so she caught her a nice mess of trout. Along about four o'clock the pack horse come in for her duffle. I bid her goodbye with no regrets and started back for Chimney Pond.

I got to Basin Pond towards evening and I found the worst mess of blowdowns I ever saw. The trail was full of trees — lengthways, sideways, crossways, every way you could imagine. I says, "That's funny! No wind down to the lake, but there must have been a whirlwind or a hurricane struck up here around the mountain!"

Bright and early the next morning I took my saw and axe, and I went back down and sawed out the old logs and clawed brush and cut roots. I worked just like a dog for two days and at the end of the second day I got my trail cleared out again through to Chimney Pond. When I got back to camp that second evening I found old Pamola sitting there on a rock waiting for me. He was looking a good bit healthier than when I last seen him, but he still looked pretty run-down and tuckered out.

I says, "Good evening, friend, what can I do for you?"

"Do!" he says, "Young man, you've done enough! I can't seem to keep you out of here, so maybe I'm resigned to that, but IF YOU EVER BRING THAT WOMAN IN HERE AGAIN I'LL THROW THE WHOLE FOREST OVER THAT TRAIL SO YOU'LL NEVER GET THROUGH!"

"SPIDER" EMERTON[7]

One of the first parties I took to the mountain was one man alone. One day he come to town looking for a guide to take him to the mountain. All the old guides was busy or else scared of carrying a heavy load, so they sent him to me. His name was Emerton and he was a scientist, expert in spiders and such. He came to me and asked me if I thought I could find my way through to the mountain. I told him I could. He says, "What you say you and I try it?" Of course I was as pleased as a dog with two tails.

"Now, young feller," he says, "I'll tell you: it's a long ways up there and we've got to rough it!" I told him I was ready for anything. Of course I thought he meant camping out without blankets, sleeping under old logs and behind rocks. The food question never entered my mind. I had just eaten a hearty dinner. He says, "We'll pull out and go to the river this afternoon" — which was eight miles distance.

So that night we stopped at the old Patterson place on the bank of the East Branch of the Penobscot, right where Camp Lunksoos is now. In the morning we got an early start — went up the Wassatacook Stream. I noticed our packs was uncommon light. That night we camped at Katahdin Lake and had a nice mess of trout for our supper.

So the next morning we started for Chimney Pond. He kept saying, "What beautiful country!" There was tall spruce and pine on all sides, with the very green, mossy bottoms, where now there's nothing but burnt land, poplar and white birch. Late that afternoon we reached Chimney Pond. He says, "Where are we going to camp here?"

---

7. Emerton, James Henry, WHO'S WHO IN AMERICA, 1905, and APPALACHIA, Vol. XVIII, No. 3, June, 1931, *In Memoriam*, pp. 305-306.]

I says, "We'll go across the pond to the big sheltering rock and camp under it. So you see, if a storm comes up we can keep pretty dry." When we got there, we made up a bed of balsam boughs under the rock, so we was pretty snug. That night for supper we cleaned up the last of the food we'd fetched from the Patterson place.

The next morning he told me to heat up a pot of water. I did so. He says, "Now I'll show you what our rations is going to be. Fill a couple cups of hot water and bring 'em here." Then he took a small jar out of his pack, and a spoon, and put a spoonful from the jar into my cup and the same into his own. It was a kind of a dark looking thick liquid-like. I didn't know but what it was wolf poison, but I made up my mind to try it. I asked him what it was. He says, "The extract of beef, and it is very satisfying." So I drank it and my coffee and said nothing as I wanted to be a tough guy, but I didn't really relish it. I was looking for him to pass out something else, but there was nothing more to come. He got up and stretched himself and says, "We're ready to climb the mountain and start to work."

So we clim up on the Saddle and he started making his collections of insects. He was having a fine time, too, running around the table-land, happy as a puppy. He'd spot a spider or some such and pounce on it and put it in one of his little bottles. Then he'd disappear behind a boulder and come up again corking another little bottle, just tickled to death with all he was finding.

Meantime I commenced browsing off the Alpine blueberries and cranberries along the trail. Sometimes I'd find some little insect, no bigger'n a mosquito. I'd ask him what it was and his answer would always be either, "It's a very rare specimen," or, "It's very common," and then the name he'd put on it would break an elephant's back to carry! So we worked up to about lunch time. By then I'd been hungry for about two hours.

I says, "Ain't it about time we was having lunch?"

He says, "I don't know but what it is." He looked at his watch and says, "Twenty minutes past one." Then he reached his hand back in his pocket, took out a bottle, shook out a couple pills, passed them to me and took two himself. He says, "These pills contain all the nourishment required by the human body." Then he started right off again hunting insects. I stood with my eyes and mouth wide open gazing after him!

So he finished the rest of the afternoon making his collection of insects, and he said he found some very rare specimens. About five o'clock we went back to the rock shelter to get ready for the night. I was so hungry by that time my heart was beating over on the right side. As soon's I got the fire built and some water hung on for our coffee, he says, "Get the skillet and we'll have some bacon."

Bacon never sounded so good to me before! You can bet I wa'nt very long getting the skillet out. During that time he had cut a couple slices of bacon. He passed them to me and says, "Cook 'em!" I did so, and after I'd cooked them they was no bigger than a Canadian silver five-cent piece. Then he gave me a cup of steaming hot coffee with a piece of pilot bread about three inches across and we sat down to have our supper.

After we ate, to tell you the truth, I was hungrier than before I ate anything. I'd kept still all the while, wanting to be a tough guy, but I couldn't stand it no longer without saying something. I asked him how long he thought a person could live on that kind of food before he'd starve to death. He says, "Young feller, let me show you the food value in what we've had for our supper!" He picked up a piece of birch bark, a foot-and-a-half across it both ways, took out a pencil, and begun figuring until he'd covered it all over with writing. Then he commenced to explain. I knew more before he started than after he got through.

So the next morning we started and clim the mountain again, going from the Saddle to the Peak. We come to the Brickyard. That's that bed of fine rocks part-way up to the Peak. Emerton, he spied one of them black spiders that inhabit the top of the mountain. The spider scampered down amongst the rocks and he says, "Dig over some of them for that's a lovely specimen! I must have him for my collection." So I dug ten foot off the top o' Katahdin and found the poor little spider. He sprinkled some powder on him and says, "What a lovely specimen!" Then he took a piece of paper, looked like a sweat bee's nest,[8] wrapped the spider up in it, and put it into his case he had to carry insects in. About that time I was so hungry I wa'nt no thicker than a herring! Still he kept on gathering insects, so I kept on browsing.

For five days that's the way we lived and when we got back to the East Branch of the Penobscot, I looked across and see the buildings and it was a grand sight for me! Whilst we was standing there he says to me, "We had plenty to eat whilst we'se up there, didn't we!"

I says, "You might have had, but I never so near starved in my life!"

"Well," he says, "I could walk clean to Stacyville without touching a mouthful of food."

I says, "I suppose I could, too, but I hain't going to!"

So when we got across to the house and washed up a bit the bell rang for dinner. As it was a woodsman's stopping place the food was piled right out on the table in great quantities. Believe me, it was a glad sight! So we set down and I ate till I was afraid I'd make myself sick, so I got up and left the table. Emerton, he sat and ate for a good half-hour after I got through. When he come out I says to him, "You didn't act much like a hungry man!"

"You know," he says, "that food did taste all-fired good!"

I says, "I wonder why it should?"

---

8. Sweat Bee *(Halictus sp.)* See Zim, Herbert S. PhD, and Clarence Cottam, PhD, INSECTS, Golden Press, New York, 1951.]

PAMOLA'S BRIDE

After I'd been coming in here a few years I began to see more groups like church groups and school classes and college outing clubs coming in. Almost every summer some troop of Boy or Girl Scouts would climb the mountain, and the place began to be pretty popular. Early on there was a group of school girls come in with their teachers. They were from a fancy boarding school down in Massachusetts.

In those days it was still a long ways to walk in here so there wasn't any little girls in this group, only big ones. They was quite a good looking, lively crew, especially the two lady teachers. Well, they stayed about four days here at Chimney Pond and they clim all over the mountain. Now it seemed as though whilst they was here, Pamola got his eye on them. This must have got him to thinking about ladies in a different way than he had before, because after they was gone he come flapping down to my shelter and took it up with me.

He says, "I've been very nice to you, letting you stay around up here, and I've put up with your parties coming in to climb the mountain, but I'm getting lonesome. To tell the truth I'd like me a girl to keep me company. So to pay your way, I want you to get me a girl. Now I'll give you a week to find me a girl and if you hain't got one in just one week I'm GOING TO DRIVE YOU OUT FOR SURE and I'll pile the whole forest in that trail so you'll never get back, neither!"

He said that and the next minute he was gone. Well, that was a Saturday, and I sat by the fire thinking, "How in the world am I going to get a girl for that old feller?" I felt pretty well discouraged. I didn't feel like doing anything around the camp; just moped around, for I knew Pamola'd keep his word. Saturday passed and Sunday came and went and nobody came up the trail. It was nice weather, too. Monday came and still no one came. Tuesday and Wednesday went by and not a soul was on the trail.

19

Thursday it rained, but when it came Friday and not one person had come in, I began to pack my duffle. I says, "The week'll be up tonight and I've got to get out of here."

About four o'clock I was sitting there gazing up towards Pamola Peak and the Knife Edge and thinking how much I hated to leave the place, when all at once there was a sound struck my ears. It was coming up the trail; a scraping and scratching and grinding coming up over the granite rock: clacketty-thump, thumpetty-clack! I listened for a moment and I says, "There! Somebody's coming in with a pack horse. Probably I can get them to take my equipment right out."

So I sat there and I kept looking to see the horse's head coming around the bushes, but instead of a pack horse, here came this big homely woman!

She was over six foot tall. Her hair, done up in two big braids, hung down over her shoulders, with a pink bow-ribbon on each end and a big blue bow on top of her head. Her nose was thin and sharp and hooked down and her chin was picked[9] and curled up so she could hold a cracker between her nose and chin and eat it and 'twouldn't bother her a bit. She had just two teeth left, one upper and one lower, and they passed by one another when she shut her mouth. She had a long thin neck and rust spots all over her face, some as big as my pipe bowl. I looked down at her feet. She had on about number twelve men's shoes with the soles so thick they had railroad spikes drove through them for hobnails. She carried a big pack basket and a stout yellow-birch walking stick to help her along.

I says to myself, "Well, she hain't much but perhaps she'll do." So I says to her, "What's your name?"

And she says, "My name is Sukey Guildersleeves."

"Are you alone?"

"Yes," she says, "I'm a single woman. I travel alone. I have no one to travel with me."

"Well," I says, "You must be tired."

"Oh," she says, "I'm awful tired."

I says, "I should think you might be hungry."

She says, "I'm very near famished."

"Well," I says, "You just sit right down here while I get you something to eat."

So she sat down and I got the skillet and the little kettles on over the fire and soon I had a feed of vittles on the table. She sat down and started eating. I wanted to tell her about Pamola, but I didn't know how. I never was much of a hand to talk with the ladies.

Finally I says to her, "It's a wonder to me that a good-looking woman like you should live alone, as many men as there are looking after wives."

---

9. Peaked

"Oh," she says, real pleased and curling her hair with her hands, "Is there a man here looking for a wife?"

"Oh yes," I says, "There's a man lives here in the mountain, just crazy for a wife."

She says, "How far does he live from here?"

I says, "About five minutes walk."

She jumped up from the table and says to me, "What you say we go see him?"

I says, "As soon as you finish your supper, we'll go."

"Oh," she says, "I hain't hungry!"

So we took a walk down to the end of the pond, and when we came to where all the big boulders are, I pounded on a big slab of rock that was there and Pamola slid down over the ledges and came down to where we were. He stood there rolling his eyes down on her, his arms folded and his beard blowing in the wind. She was looking up at him, skinning her teeth and looking some pleased.

I says to her, "What do you think of him?"

She looks up at him and says, "He's a man, aint he!"

I says, "Pamola, here's your girl."

He says, "Fine!" and he gives me a slap on the shoulder. "Things is all right between you and me now."

So I came back to camp and let them get acquainted. Later on, Sukey came back to camp too and settled in to stay while she and Pamola got to know each other better. I noticed she couldn't cook a bit. I had to do all the cooking. I worried a little about that. I didn't know what Pamola would think of me getting him a bride that couldn't cook, but I kept quiet and watched developments.

Every day Sukey would take a walk down to the end of the pond, and I could hear the two of them talking together most of the afternoon. Finally, after about a week, the day came when Pamola flew down and scooped her up and flew up to his cave with her. I listened to hear if there was any screeching or yelling from Sukey. I didn't hear a hint o' protest so I figured things were going just fine. I felt pretty good, so I got back to work making a clearing to build me a cabin here.

The next morning I was out in the yard, digging out rocks and stones, happy as a clam at high water, when all at once I heard an awful commotion over toward the North Peaks. It didn't sound like thunder, but more like big boulders tunking and bumping around. Now and again it would sound like a slide of boulders rolling down a steep cliff. I listened to it for a while, but finally curiosity got the best of me and I had to go see what it was. I started right out in the hot sun and I clim the side of Hamlin Ridge, about half a mile. When I got to the top I could see the North Peak. There was Pamola with the largest garden rake I ever saw, and he was rolling the big rocks into the valley.

I went over there and I says, "What on earth are you doing making all this racket?"

"Why," says Pamola, "I'm making a smooth place for us to push the baby carriage." So I could see that things was going real well.

"Now, that's just fine," I says, "Yes, sir!" And if you go over to the North Peaks now you can see where Pamola raked it all nice and smooth.

Well, things went on pretty smooth for about three days. Then one morning bright and early I heard Pamola's voice and I could tell he was angry! So I listened to see what he was saying.

He says, "YOU QUEERED THE WHOLE THING! YOU'VE RAISED THE DEUCE WITH THE WHOLE WORKS!" Then I heard a rumble. It sounded like a landslide. The next thing I see was his woman. She appeared out of the bushes and says, "I wunt live with that old devil! I weeded his whiskers in good shape this morning. I'm leavin!" And away she went down the trail, thumpetty-clack, thumpetty-clack, only faster'n when she come up. She didn't even stop for her pack basket.

Now I was needing a bucket of water. So I took my bucket, the only one I had, walked down to the shore of the pond and stepped out on a rock. I could feel quite a breeze blowing as I stooped to dip my water up. When I dipped the bucket, the water come into it with such force it was pulled out of my hand and away it went around the edge of the pond: tunkety-tunk-tunk,

23

tunkety-tunk-tunk against the rocks. My pipe fell out of my mouth! I stood there staring at the water to see what caused it. Then I happened to cast my eyes up onto the big ledge on the side of the mountain. There stood Pamola and in his hands he held this thing like a big dust broom. He was swinging it around and around and it seemed as though the water in the pond was following it.

As I stood there watching it I saw the water drawing away from the shore. It kept getting higher and higher in the middle, till every drop of water in the pond was in one great big ball. Now that ball was spinning at about a thousand revolutions a minute and making a "swish-ka-swish" as it went around. Then Pamola reached this big dust broom down, touched it and give it a flop. That sent every bit of it into Basin Pond, a mile and a half away. I had to carry water from there for two weeks in a quart bottle. The last day I walked over toward the second pond and I found my bucket, all dented up, lying there on the shore.

FIFTEEN FRY PANS ON THE WALL

One day a man blew into camp and he told me he was writing a book concerning Mt. Katahdin. He asked me if I'd tell him something about the mountain. I told him I'd tell him all I knew and it wouldn't take me long to do it. So he stayed around and explored and evenings we talked about the mountain.

One day when he'd been around a few days, my wife and I were going out to get some wood. He says, "Let me go out and help cut that wood." I told him he'd better stay to camp as I'd pulled my arms outa joint the day before hauling a fella on the crosscut saw. "Maybe," he says, "you think I can't use a saw." I told him that's just what I thought. "Well," he says, "I'll go out with ye and show ye!" And I told him if he was no good he'd come back to camp, too.

So when we got out there he got hold of the saw and he could saw as good as I could! After we'd got the wood sawed he says, "What'd ye think of me now?" I told him I guessed he'd pass.

After he'd been here about a week and I'd been telling him all about the mountain, he was standing in front of the stove one night, and he noticed all the fry pans hanging up back of the stove. He asked me, "Where'd you get all them fry pans?"

I says, "You wunt believe me if I tell you."

Says he, "I don't know. I been believing a lot of the stuff you been tellin me!"

"Well," I says, "a party come up here one time, clim the mountain and cruised around. One day, whilst they was out cruising they caught a partridge and brought it into camp. They thought it would make a nice pet and to keep it from flying away whilst they was up climbing the mountain, they took their frying pan and tied it to its leg. They had him three or four days, and they thought he was gettin real tame.

"Then one night they come in after a hard day's climb and they commenced to look for their bird so's to feed him his supper.

25

They hunted high and low but they couldn't find him. By that time their vacation was up and they had to start for home. I hunted for the bird for a while after they'd gone, but I couldn't find it. Finally summer was gone and I bid goodbye to Chimney Pond till the next spring.

"The following summer I wanted a straight pole to fix up around the camp so I went out in the woods to cruise for one and I run onto a flock of partridge, about fifteen of them. And judge my surprise when I found each one with a fry pan on his leg!

"After I had taken the fry pan off the first two, the others seemed so rejoiced they come right to me and held their feet up for me to take the fry pans off! Instead of getting the pole I went after, I picked up an armful of fry pans and lugged them into camp. They's right here now to show for themselves."

THE MAN WITH THE GREEN HAT

I can't think of his name but I'll call him the Man with the Green Hat. This was back about 1931. I had a party of young folks with their professor. They wanted to see the whole mountain and to look at the geology. This one feller, he told me how he'd clim the Matterhorn in Switzerland, had scaled the lofty walls of Mt. McKinley and Mt. Hood without making a misstep, and was planning a trip up Mt. Everest. He says, "I'm terribly disappointed in Katahdin, for I've thought by the tales I've heard and the reading I've read that it was a mountain. But it looks to me just like an ant hill."

Well, I couldn't say much because Katahdin was the only mountain I'd ever clim myself. I told him I thought it was quite a mountain. He was the first feller I ever saw that wore those funny leather shorts they wear in Switzerland, and he had this kind of CUTE little green hat, with a red feather stuck in it.

Next thing, we was getting ready to go and I was putting up sandwiches for lunch. He says, "You needn't put up any for me. I've always lived on dry fruit when I climb mountains." So he filled his pockets with dried apples, dried apricots, dried pears, prunes, raisins and dried peaches till his pockets stuck out like a chipmunk's jaws. Then we all started out and he commenced nibbling just about as soon as we left the camp.

He ate continually and by the time we got to Index Rock, he was starting to think about a drink of water. "Well," I says, "there's a little spring just down back of the summit. We can probably get you a drink when we get over there."

When we got to the notch between Pamola and Chimney Peaks, which goes about a hundred feet straight down on one side, then a flat bottom of about twenty feet and another hundred feet straight up, he looked at it .

He says, "That looks pretty bad."

I says, "It ain't as bad as it looks."

27

I noticed he was standing on the rock and not following me, so I asked if he didn't want me to help him down. He says, "If you're a mind to. It's a strange trail to me. You know where the foot holds are." So I took hold of his feet and placed them in the notches in the rocks and showed him where to take hold with his hands. I noticed his knees was shaking some, so I worked him up Chimney Peak the same way. He stuck out his chest and says, "That's nothing to compare with the Matterhorn!"

So we all started along and when we come to a narrow place on the Knife Edge I turned to see how he was making it. Lo and behold, he was down astraddle of it, hanging on with both hands and hitching along about six inches to a hitch. When we'd come to a smooth place in the trail, down would go his hand into his pocket and out would come the dried fruit. Into his mouth it went: the raisins, prunes, apricots, pears, and when we come to another narrow place, the hitching process would start up again.

Finally we reached Baxter Peak and he says, "I'm terribly disappointed. It ain't half the mountain I thought it was. I'm getting awful thirsty! Is there any water handy?"

I says, "There's some in a spring about thirty rod away. There's almost always water there if it isn't dried up. Of course it's been a pretty dry time, this spring."

He turned around and looked at the sun. He says, "Does the sun rise in the east here?"

I told him I supposed it did.

He says, "It looks to me as though it rises in the north."

I says, "By the looks it's going to be a long hot day. We'll feel the effect of it before we get to Hamlin Peak."

"Oh, but," he says, "if we had a drink of cold water I'd be all right!" The other boys didn't say nothing, but they kept looking and winking.

So we started down to where the spring is, but not a drop of water was there in it. Now the professor wanted the boys to see the whole top of the mountain, so I says, "Maybe we'll find water in Thoreau Spring," and we headed for there. I saw that this feller's tongue was kinda hanging out, but I pretended not to notice. The other boys seemed to be doing all right.

It only took us about twenty minutes to get to Thoreau Spring, but when we arrived, there wasn't a sign of water there, either. By then this feller's tongue was commencing to hang down on his shirt front and some of the others were beginning to feel a mite thirsty, too. So we took the cut-off over to Saddle Spring. The little feller with the green hat was really suffering by now, but he was still taking a piece of dry fruit now and again to keep up his strength.

Well sir, Saddle Spring was dry, too, and this feller was beginning to sound desperate. "Isn't there any water anywhere?" he says. Now the professor wanted the boys to look over the Klondike and the Northwest Basin before they came back to camp, so I says, "We're going over to Caribou Spring next. That hardly ever runs dry. We'll eat our lunch at Caribou Spring," I says.

"I don't have to stop to eat my lunch," he says, "I eat as I go along. That's the good part of it!" He was still chewing away at a steady chew as he walked along, for he had a good supply with him: about two pounds of raisins and two of apricots, not to mention the dried apples and dried pears and prunes and whatnot. He says, "Will it take us very long to get there? I've just got to have some water pretty soon!"

"Well," I says, "you can go on ahead of us. The trail's easy to follow." So I showed him the trail to Caribou Spring, told him what to look for and sent him off ahead of the rest of us. I never should have done that. A man should always keep his party together, especially when there are greenhorns, but I felt sorry for the feller by now, he looked so pitiful with his tongue hanging out for water, and he said how he was an old mountaineer!

So that feller, he took off across the tableland at a jog and the rest of us trailed along behind. We could see his little green hat with the red feather in it bobbing along ahead of us through the scrub most of the way till he disappeared over the rise just this side of the spring.

We all clim for a few more minutes toward the top of the

ridge, when all to once — PBLUG — they was a huge sound like dynamite going off in deep water. We all set out for the spring on the dead run! We couldn't think what had happened. When we got to the spring there was plenty of water, but we couldn't find the feller with the green hat anywhere abouts. The only sign of him we ever found was his little green hat with the red feather sticking in it, sitting there on the boulder beside the spring.

The next week I was out to Millinocket to get some supplies and I went around and talked to the doctor about it. The doctor told me it was a severe case of Double-Barreled Indigestion.

PEPPER TEA

Well, I'm going to tell you how I made friends with old Pamola. Now I used to have to make my rounds regular over to Daicey Pond, and Kidney Pond, visiting York's and Bradeen's camps over on the west side of Katahdin. Well, one time it was getting quite late and looking like rain. I thought I better be getting back to Chimney Pond before nightfall. But when I got on top of the mountain the wind come up and the rain come down in sheets.

So I arrived at the cabin just a little after dark, cooked my supper and done the dishes. Then I got out an old Western novel and sat down by the table to read a while by candlelight. The storm was raging something terrific outside. I could hear the wind whistling around Pamola Peak and the Knife Edge and over towards the Chimney, making a groaning noise like so many dying people. I sat there reading. The great big fir trees were bending, their tops lashing together, and hail struck on the roof as big as hens' eggs. Everything outside looked as though it was turned upside-down. I could hear the roofing flopping back and forth and the boards slamming back. I was expecting every moment to hear the roof go off the camp and be left there sitting in the rain.

All of a sudden I heard something strike the ground awful heavy out in the yard. I thought it was one of the big trees had blowed down, so I paid little attention to it. I kept on at the book, and first thing I heard was an awful groan that made the teakettle dance on the stove. I stopped reading and sat still for a minute, staring at the window. Soon it was followed by another groan. I listened and I says, "That sounds funny. I'll see what that is."

So I got up and went into the back room and got my revolver. I rolled the cylinder around to see that it was full of new cartridges. Then I took the flashlight and stepped to the door.

31

About that time there come another groan and when I threw open the door, such a sight met my gaze I shall never forget! For lying on his back, stretched out full length in the yard lay old Pamola with both hands grasping his stomach.

I says, "What is the trouble, Pamola?"

He says, "I went down to Sandy Stream Pond and killed a tough old cow moose and ate the whole of her and I think I overdone the thing a little bit! U-U-UGH-H-M-M-M-M!" Then came another awful groan.

I says, "I'll see what I can do to help you." I didn't have much stuff for doctoring indigestion, but I couldn't see Pamola lie there and suffer so.

I went into the camp. I had a bucket of water there, still on the stove and hot, so I put in about two pounds of sugar, to sweeten it up good, and put in a pound of black pepper. I stirred it up well, took it out and gave it to Pamola. He drank it at one big GULLUP. He commenced to rub his stomach. Soon he straightened up and says, "I'm feeling better." He got up, stretched himself and says, "You've taken the cramp out of my stomach! I'll be a true, honest, faithful friend to you as long as I live. I'll never do anything more to harm ye!"

He flopped his wings and flew towards his den, and Pamola and I have been the best of friends ever since. And I always keep a good supply of Pepper Tea in camp, for I don't know when I might want to use it.

PAMOLA'S WINTER HOME

Come winter, I didn't get to the mountain much. I was working as a deputy warden for the Fish and Game and I was on the
go from one place to another, roaming around through the woods
on foot. I had to visit the lumber camps and watch the trappers
and see that they didn't violate the game laws. I had the district
all around to the north and east of the mountain.

Now there was an old bear trapper that camped at a lake not a
great ways from the mountain. He used to slaughter deer and
moose to bait his bear traps. So in March when the snow was
deep and a deer is easy killed with a hunting knife, he went up to
his camp to prepare for the spring hunt.

After he'd been up there about a week the chief warden told
me to go up to see what he was doing, whether he was killing any
deer or not. When I arrived at his camp he wa'nt very friendly,
but I stayed on just the same. I cruised around all the snowshoe
tracks I found leading out of camp and found no sign of a deer
kill. Then one day I wandered over to Sandy Stream Pond and
just below the pond by a bog I came to where a moose had been
killed. There was moose tracks and blood and hair and plenty of
sign of an awful scuffle in the snow, so I started looking for
snowshoe tracks. Instead of finding any snowshoe tracks, I found
three long claw marks, resembling a giant eagle's footprint.

The moose seemed to have been picked right up and carried
away whole, but by the streaks of blood on the snow I was able to
follow him. He seemed to be headed straight for the mountain. I
followed along. The trail seemed to go right toward Cathedral
Rock. That's that ledge there, that sticks up about five hundred
feet perpendicular, just to the right of Chimney Pond. Right at the
foot of the rock they's a couple acres of scrub, and in this scrub
was a little, small clearing where the moose had been dropped,
and again I could see the eagle-like footprints in the snow. There
was a dark hole in under this ledge, and it seemed as though the

moose had been dragged right towards this hole. I had my big flashlight so I made up my mind to follow along in a ways and see what become of the moose. The path seemed to be well wore.

So I took off my snowshoes and stuck them up in the snow beside the doorway, there. Then I had myself a little taste out of my canteen. That made me feel warmer and gave me a bit more courage. Then, with my flashlight in one hand and revolver in the other, I headed into the passage.

Well, I hadn't gone but a little ways in under the rock when I heard the noise. It sounded like someone was striking a tight cable with a heavy iron bar: TUMM...TUMMM...TUMMMMM. I checked my revolver again, just to see it was well loaded, before I ventured further. After going in about ten rods I come to a large room which was filled up with dried bones piled up like cord wood. TUMM...TUMMM...TUMMMMM! That kept getting louder and louder. After I'd traveled nearly a quarter of a mile under the mountain, I looked ahead and I see a pale light. That thumping noise was almost deafening! TUMM! TUMMM! TUM-MMMM!

Finally I come to a point of ledge which projected out in the path. As I rounded the corner of it I spied where the light was coming from. A big white boulder was in one corner shining brightly and sending its light to other big boulders which reflect-ed light all over the cave.

Right in the center of this room, on a big stone chair that'd weigh all of twenty ton, sat old Pamola with the biggest violin that I ever saw. The noise I'd heard had been him tuning it up, drawing his thumb across the strings. As I stood and watched him he seemed to get it pretty well tuned up, so he picked up his bow, full twenty foot long, drawed it across the strings, and the sound nearly took my head off! But it seemed as though he had it all in good tune.

Next I saw Pamola reach out one of those long toes of his, place it in a loop that was hanging down in front of him. When he pulled down on the loop I saw a rock that weighed as much as four ton rise right up and come down, KA-BANG, against a big flat slab. Next thing I saw, out of a dark passageway come just the skeleton of an Indian, with his long black hair sticking to his snow-white bones. Again that huge rock swung up and struck TWO and out come a second Indian. It kept on that way till they was thirteen skeleton Indians in the room. It was the ghostliest sight I ever saw in my life!

Then Pamola picked up his bow and started to play. I don't know what tune it was, unless it was the Devil's Dream. The Indians joined right in a dance 'round in a circle. They was going, "A HIDDEN AN' A HAW! A HAW AN' A HIDDEN!" They had things in their hands, looked like short horns, that they was hitting down on their thighs— where their thighs should be— they was nothing but dry bones.

Pamola, he danced them around for about one half hour. Then he hooked his toe in that loop again and pulled. Up went the big rock and struck thirteen times. The last Indian skeleton to come out was the first to go back in. Next, Twelve, and in goes another. Next time, Eleven; in goes another one. Next time, Ten and another one disappeared behind the rock. Then Nine, and then Eight, and I commenced to think it's about time for me to be moving!

I come to the mouth of the cave and put on my snowshoes. Believe me, there was no grass grew under my feet between there and Katahdin Lake! It was a good while before I wanted to visit Pamola's winter home again.

HOW I TURNED THE FEVER

One winter night back home in Stacyville, I was sleeping and having awful dreams! It seemed as though Pamola was in great trouble. Then I'd wake up. When I'd drop off in another drowse, I'd see Pamola again, suffering with great pain. So when morning came, it was on my mind and worried me so that I got out my snowshoes, packed up my pack basket and made for Pamola's winter home. It took me two days to get all the way to the opening in the ledges where you go in. When I started into the passage I thought of the last time I'd come here but I was getting more worried. There wa'nt no tracks in the snow around the doorway, same's there'd ought to be. So into the cave I went.

After I'd passed the room with the dry bones, I heard a deep groan. I knew Pamola was in great pain, so I continued on to his sleeping quarters. There was Pamola in a raging fever! I knew then that my dreams were sent to me, on purpose, to help him out of his troubles.

Amongst the medicine I had brought I had a large bottle of aconite and I knew it was good to stop a fever. For a person all it takes is a few drops in a glass of water. Pamola was so large, I give him a pint in ten quarts of water. I held it up and he drank every bit of it. Then he whispered and says, "Dear friend, you know, I'm a mighty sick man."

Well, I started in doctoring him up. I took red pepper and dry mustard that I fetched in my pack, and I mixed it up in a paste and plastered it over his lungs and around his throat, for I was afraid he might have pneumonia. Then I started a fire, het up a couple good rocks, and rolled them over to his feet.

He complained about his knees aching and told me to do something for them. Of course I couldn't rub them hard enough to stop the pain, so I gathered up some rocks as big as a quart dipper, stood back a few paces and pelted them at his knees. Every time a rock would hit, Pamola'd say, "WHAT A RELIEF!" All night long I sat by his bedside and it fetched tears to my eyes to see him lie there on that bed of pain.

Three nights I stayed there, doctoring him, and the third night the fever started to turn. The trouble was it would turn about halfway, then go back again. Then it would start and go about halfway, then back again. I could see right off something had to be done. So I grabbed right hold of it with both hands and laid on all my strength. It started to turn and I got it a little over halfway around, when it give a SNAP and back it went! I went flying across the cave, struck up against the rocks and lay there stunned for five minutes.

When I come to, I was good'n mad! Old Pamola was lying there rolling his eyes and scarcely breathing. I grabbed hold of that fever again with both hands, determined to twist her this time. I laid on every ounce of strength and I got it past the halfway mark! Soon it commenced to go easier, and when it did get started turning, how it did buzz around, and me hanging on for dear life! I must of ridden around on it five hundred times and such an awful thrashing I got! Finally it was gone. It left me sitting on the floor with a bump on my head as big as a good big apple. I sat there dazed. What fetched me out was Pamola's voice. He was saying, "IT'S GONE!"

I looked, and there he was, setting up.

He says to me, "You're one of the greatest doctors in the world!"

I says, "Yes, but I'll have nothing more to do with turning fevers!" I says, "Some people is so narrow that the fever can't turn on 'em! Here I am, a total wreck!"

PAMOLA'S BATH

One night Pamola was setting on the peak looking at the beautiful moon. I see him come out on his favorite roosting place on the big ledge. He beckoned for me to come up. So I clim up the face of the rock and got up to where he was standing. He took and boosted me up on a large boulder, set down beside me and says, " You know you've done me a great favor and relieved my suffering. Tomorrow night I'm going to take my bath. When I get that done I'll feel like myself again."

I told him I was planning to go over to the Northwest Basin, the next day, to see how my shelter was doing and see if the porcupine had et it up. He says, "If you want any help, call on me. Shake hands," he says, "for we are friends hereafter."

Well just after dark the next night I was up on the big ledge back of Lake Cowles in the Northwest Basin when I heard a thundering of wings. It was Pamola. I saw his two bright eyes coming over the scrub headed straight for the shore of Lake Cowles. On Pamola's back was a heavy sack filled with something, I didn't know what it was. He lugged it down to the foot of the pond and spread it around. I see it was nothing but rocks off'n the Old Man's slide. He had about half an acre, all covered over with that coarse gravel. I says, "That's the queerest performance I ever see." So I watched him.

"Now," he says, "the big round knoll, there, is my cushion where I sit and soak my feet. I take a great deal of comfort out of that."

Then Pamola got ready. First he laid down in the pond and got wet all over. Then he come to his bed of gravel. He lay down and he rolled over and he rubbed it on himself and he rubbed it in! Then he reached up and grabbed one of the bog spruces, there, with a thick top, pulled it up, root and all, scoured his back, scoured around under his arms and up and down his legs, and in back of his ears. He used it especially to scratch between his horns. Finally he got all scrubbed and he stood on the bank and he made a big plunge for the pond. Ka-PLUG!

Well, I wasn't looking for anything like that, but there was a regular tidal wave come out of the pond and took me clean in under the arms! If I hadn't of grabbed hold of a tree there, and hung on, it would of washed me clean down over the mountain. Pamola looked up and he says, "Well, dear friend, I didn't calculate to do anything like that to ye!"

He rolled and he scrubbed in the water, there, for as much as an hour. Every once in a while he'd put on a new supply of gravel. Finally he got up and rubbed himself around on the bushes and trees till he got all dried off.

"Now," he says, "I'm going back to camp. Would you like to go with me?" He stroked his beard.

I says, "I certainly would."

"Well," he says, "I'll carry you over."

I got on Pamola's back and he riz them big wings and away he flew. When he come over the tableland he lowered down just so as his beard would drag in the little scrub spruce trees there and away he went, combing his whiskers and leaving a trail of dust behind same's you'd see behind a thrashing machine.

He says, "You just see how nice that beard feels, now." I grabbed hold of his beard. Why it felt just as soft as a baby's hair. 'Twas just as lovely! "Now," he says, "you know I feel a good deal better. I've had my bath and I feel like a man. I love that Lake Cowles and the big round knoll where I can sit and soak my feet with no one to bother me. I think that's the best place in the world to bathe in."

Now any time you're over to the Northwest Basin on a Saturday night you'll be likely to see him, soaking his feet or setting in the water of Lake Cowles, whistling the *Battle Hymn of the Republic* and scrubbing his back with a spruce tree. He don't miss too many Saturdays.

THE FAT MAN FROM BOSTON

It was in the month of August. The weather'd been so dry there wasn't a breath of air stirring and there hadn't been for a week. Everthing was getting dry and we was scared of forest fire. Well, I was sitting on the porch this one day, looking up at the mountain. The sun was there, a great ball of fire shining in the heavens.

As I sat looking and looking at the headwall, there, and wishing for rain, I see up the trail there was a man coming. He was short and fat, so as he put me in mind of one of these roly poly dolls. Every step was a GRUNT or a PUFF. The sweat was streaming down his cheeks and in his hand he carried a red bandana, mopping his face as he came along.

Well, he come up to the porch. "Hello, Hello!" he says, "Here I am! I've got this far, anyway. The people told me I was too fleshy to climb Mt. Katahdin, but I've got this far! When I make up my mind to do a thing I 'most always do it," he says, "and I've made up my mind to go up Katahdin! I don't care if I don't get clean to the peak," he says, "I'll get up where I can get a view of the country, see what it looks like and see these lakes and ponds they've told me so much about." So he talked on for a few minutes, wiping the sweat from his brow. Finally he says, "If you'll give me a chance to bed down for the night I'll rest and make the climb tomorrow."

I says, "Come in and make yourself right to home. If you want to cook on the stove, there's the dishes; use 'em. Act just as though you owned the place. You can have the under bunk in the northwest corner of the camp. So he took his pack and went into the back room. Pretty soon he come out with his arms full of tin cans and paper bags and cooked his supper.

He says, "I'm kind of dieting to get rid of some of this flesh I got on." I can swear he et for his supper as much as I ever see! After supper I commenced to tell him some stories and pleased

43

him so he burst out laughing and when he did he shook all over like a dish of Jello. So I kept him laughing till bedtime for I was getting a big kick out of him.

When the morning come, he had his breakfast and got ready to make the climb. I told him about the Chimney Notch and how difficult it is getting people across from Pamola Peak to Chimney Peak. I told him, some people, I almost had to carry over.

He says, "How do you work it with big fleshy persons like me?"

"I take 'em apart," I told him, "and carry 'em across one chunk to a time and put 'em together on the other side." He tipped his head back and gave a laugh that jarred two panes of glass out of the cabin window!

"Well," he says, "here goes it!" and he started off up the trail to Pamola Peak. Now that trail's rocky and steep, and it was an awful hot day. The fat man was very stout; his stomach projected right out over his belt. When he got as far as the Index Rock it was so awful hot he was puffing and blowing like a porpoise. He was afraid his heart would play out. So he turned and retraced his steps back toward Chimney Pond.

Well, he sat down and rested for a while and to amuse himself he rolled some of them big rocks down over the side of the mountain just to hear them crash on the big ones below. We hollered to him not to do it, but he kept right on. Lucky there was no one else climbing behind him since they might of got killed. Anyways, every time he stopped to rest he kept doing it and pretty soon he rolled some right over Pamola's den. They went right across the mouth of the cave and little did he know what he'd done! It kind of made Pamola mad to hear them big boulders tumbling right down at his front door when he's taking his rest.

So the man come on down to the pond. Now by those days, we had a sign here saying "DRINKING WATER - NO BATHING OR WASHING," but the fat man felt awful hot and sweaty. He stood there on the shore and gazed at the clear crystal water, and it looked so inviting he thought he'd take a swim anyway. So he

44

stripped off his clothes, got in and started to swim across the pond, and that was enough for old Pamola. That fat man had done two things to make Pamola mad, and now he had given him just the chance how to get even.

Now Pamola he had a big rubber hoselike thing up there in his den, coiled up and kept on purpose for when he felt thirsty and wanted a drink without leaving the comfort of his cozy cave. So he watched for just the right moment and then he let that thing flop down over the ledges into the water and he sucked every drop of water out of that pond, leaving the fat man stranded right on top of a big picked rock out in the middle, there, hanging right on his belly with his arms and legs sticking out every which way.

Well, I was working around the camp, there, not paying much attention, when all of a sudden I heard the fat man yelling something awful, and I thought somebody must have fell in and was drownding. So I run down to the shore and I see not a drop of water in the pond and him out there on top of this big picked rock, poised right on his belly so he couldn't touch his hands or feet! I could see Pamola had a hand in this and I couldn't say as I blamed him at that. Still I couldn't leave the fat man stuck there. So I went back and hustled around and got the hammer and nails and built me a ladder and went down and took that man off'n the rock. He says, "I never see water disappear out of a pond so quick as it did out of this!"

The ladder's lying right there beside the trail, now, and every time I go after a pail of water I think of Pamola and the Fat Man on the rock.

THE WRATH OF PAMOLA

This is one of the things Pamola does when things don't go to suit him. As near as I can tell, what happened to get him mad this time was a little building. I had one sitting out back of camp and porcupine had chewed it up so as it was very uncomfortable to sit in. So one spring I thought I'd build a new one and shift it farther from the cabin.

Well, I selected a nice sunny spot out on the trail leading up to Pamola Peak, quite handy to the mountain, and things went along fine. I was putting up the walls of smooth peeled logs and doing what I thought was a real fancy job. Pamola must have been asleep or else he didn't know what I was building till I put the seats in. To make it real stylish I put white enamel on the seats, and I was working away at the window when I heard a CRACK up on the mountain. I looked up and saw the whole top of the mountain toppling over, and down it come over the side! One large rock as big as a barn come within forty feet of my new building and another large one went into the pond.

I knew Pamola was doing it to scare me. He'd promised that he wouldn't hurt me, the time I cured him of the belly-ache. So I paid no attention to the rocks coming down. I kept working at my little building, and I fixed it up fine with a door facing the west.

One day after that I went up and met old Pamola, to have a talk with him. When he saw me coming he would hardly speak. Finally he turns to me and says, "What did you do that for?"

I says, "Do what?"

He says, "Build that building out there! It's a nice sight for me, to gaze down on that flat roof!"

I says, "That won't hurt you any, Pamola."

"HURT ME, NO!" he says, "'Twunt hurt me! How'll it be when all them flies lights on my nose and in my whiskers, when I lie with my head out of the cave?" He says, "By good rights, if I

47

hadn't promised you I wouldn't do anything more to you, I'd smash that thing so it'd be flatter'n a pancake!"

"Well, Pamola," I says, "it's an awful hard job to go build another."

He says, "Since you've done it, let it go. I'll put up with it some way."

So the little building stands there, with its white logs shining through the green trees. It's so nice with the white enamel seats and everything in it, and with the door facing west so a person can look towards the Saddle and watch the beautiful sunset and see the different colors on the trees and rocks. Folks can sit there enjoying themselves, some with a book in their hand, reading long tales. Some even occupy it for an hour to a time!

I fixed it up so the trail runs right by it and people can't help but go in and try one of the soft seats. Sometimes when a person goes in there and sits a long while, Pamola comes out on top of the mountain with a crowbar to start one of them big rocks to come crashing down behind the little building. And believe me, that'll do the job!

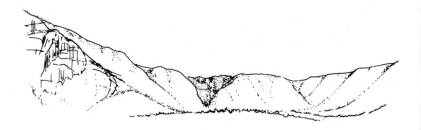

THE GROWLER

It was in the month of September. The weather was very clear and fine. All the people here had enjoyed a good climb in the mountain and were back in camp. Some of them were getting their evening meal, and all around the camp you could smell the frying bacon and the steaming coffee.

Some folks that had got in earlier were telling the adventures they'd had that day and the things they'd seen from the top of the mountain. Others had sat down to a game of bridge, whilst some of the younger boys and girls were doing a little singing down on the shore of the pond. A few were sitting on the porch admiring the beautiful sunset.

When the sun disappeared over the saddle it left a purple hue on the top of Pamola Peak. As the folks sat there watching it change from one color to another, they says, "What beautiful colors!" and, "What a spot this is!" and, "There's nothing to compare with this!" Everything seemed nice and lovely. All were enjoying themselves, and it looked as though we were going to have a splendid evening. Little did we think it would be interrupted.

But I stood on the porch and I heard voices coming up the trail. I says, "I guess we're going to have company." I kind of kept looking down the trail and sure enough, three men hove into view with quite heavy packs. The first two, I spoke to.

I says, "Hello, boys."

They says, "Hello." They looked up at the mountain.

Then came the man in the rear. He looked something like a man off in the distance; then when he got handy, you could see he hain't. He says, "All I see is MUD and ROCKS and this trail is so crooked it would break a snake's back getting up it!"

He turned to me and says, "I should think you'd get some of those rocks out of the trail before somebody falls over them and breaks a leg! I'm hungry!" he says, "Where can we cook our supper?"

I says, "You can come in and cook on the stove tonight. The fire's all going."

He looked in at the door, saw the people that were playing bridge, and says, "Looks as though this place is occupied."

I says, "Yes, but these people'll move when you get ready to have your supper."

"Well," he says, "I don't like to cook in this stifled-up hole, anyway."

So I says, "Well, you can have an open fire."

He says, "Is there a fireplace here that aint in use?"

I told him there was and there was wood all cut. Then I took him up to one of the shelters, and I says, "Boys, how does this suit ye?"

The two boys with him says, "This is fine. Can we sleep here tonight?"

I says, "Yes, you can have this as long as you stop here."

They says, "That suits us."

I says, "And there's a fresh balsam bed that I just put down today."

They felt their hand on the balsam and said, "That's grand!"

The other feller says, "I don't see nothin grand about it! It aint a fit place to keep PIGS!"

They says, "Where do you get your water from?"

I told them at the pond.

He says, "Who do you suppose is going to drink out of that bog hole?"

I says, "You can take the bucket and go down to the spring. It's only a mile down there."

The other men got the fire started, but the smoke blew around in the Growler's eyes. He says, "Yes, we'll be just like smoked hams when we get outa here!"

I'd made up my mind that he couldn't get through any too soon to please me. And I'd heard about all the growling I wanted for a while. So I went back to the cabin where the other people were and left him and his two friends to cook their supper.

Later, one of them came down into the camp after a frying

pan. He says, "That man we've got along with us, I think, is the worst growler that ever lived. There don't seem to be nothing that will satisfy him here or at home. He growls at his wife at home. We'd ought to have known better than to fetch him on this trip. He makes it disagreeable for himself and everyone."

I says, "What was he doing when you came down?"

He says, "Chewing the rag as usual."

Well, you know I kind of had sympathy for them two fellers that were with him for they seemed to be real nice men. They were out for a good time and enjoying camp life, but he seemed bent on taking all the pleasure out of it. So after they had their supper, they came down and asked me if I had some blankets for them. I told them I had a few that weren't in use and I'd bring them up. So I picked up an armful of blankets, carried them up to their shelter, and laid them down.

The Growler, he looked at them, grumbling, "No more nor less than horse blankets!"

I says, "Ought to keep a jackass warm one night!"

So I saw no more of him that night, but I could hear the mumbling and grumbling going on and I knew he was finding fault steadily, chewing the rag the whole time.

The next morning it was fine and nice and the three of them came down to the camp to ask about the trails and about what they should take with them — whether they needed a canteen to carry water in or not. I told them they'd better take water along, for it had been awful dry and springs might not have much water in them. The Growler, he says, "You boys can take what you want to, but I've climbed all the rocks that I'm going to! I can see all of this hole I want to right from here!"

I was kind of in hopes he'd go, so I'd get a little rest, but there was no such good news. He lay around all day, finding fault at everything. Even the water wasn't fit to drink. It was solid full of microbes. Then the smoke from the fire would get in his eyes. Then every little bit of rabbit droppings or birch bark he'd see around the shelters, he'd growl about that. "Why don't you bury those things somewheres, so it'll be wholesome for a person to live?" He'd see a fly crawling up the window pane. "There's more filth right there!"

And when the people began to come down off the mountain from the day's climb, he met them and commenced to find fault with the way they were dressed. They either had on too many clothes or not enough. One man got his camera out to take a picture of the mountain. The Growler says to him, "You haven't got much to do taking pictures. It looks to me just like a big pile o' rock!" The feller with the camera paid no attention to him.

A little white-throated sparrow started singing and one of the women said, "How beautiful!"

He says, "It sounds like an old rusty gate hinge!"

Then he walked around from one lean-to to the other visiting people, finding fault with first one and then the other. It seemed as though no one was doing anything to suit him. Some of the boys and girls started laughing. He says, "I don't know what you see to laugh at in this forsaken hole, no good for anything but bears and wolves!"

So the people got fairly disgusted with him. His growling and whining drove all the cheerfulness outa the camp.

Then his friends got off the mountain and told him what a lovely day they'd had, and he says, "Keep it to yourselves!"

Some of the people asked me how long was he going to stay. I says, "He's in for three days."

"Well," they says, "hain't there some way that we can get rid of him?"

I says, "Yes, but it'll cause a little hardship on the rest of you."

They says, "We're willing to stand anything to get rid of that man!"

I says, "All right, then, we'll have him out of here before tomorrow comes."

So when night came, I went up on the mountain to have a talk with old Pamola. I give the signal and Pamola came up and sat down beside me. He laid his big loving hand on my shoulder and says, "What can I do for you, dear friend?"

I says, "There's a lot you can do."

52

He says, "I heard the worst growling and grumbling down there that I ever heard in my life. Is there some kind of wild animal bothering the people?"

I says, "No, it's no wild animal. It's something that looks like a man off at a distance. When you get handy, you see he hain't."

"Oh, yes," he says, "I see."

I told him about the feller growling and grumbling so much and asked him if there was anything he could do to drive him out.

He says, "I see. You want me to give him the works. I can do it, but it'll bring a lot of hardship on the other good people that are down there."

I says, "They're willing to stand anything to get rid of that fault-finder."

He says, "I'll give him the works before twelve o'clock!"

So I bid Pamola good night and returned to the cabin. When I got there some of the young people were singing and the Growler was sitting on a rock, still chewing the rag about this and that. Finally he straightened up and says, "These blasted rocks are so hard no one can take comfort on them!" and he got up and sneaked off to his lean-to. It was a good big relief to the people to get rid of his whinniking for a while.

About eleven o'clock that night we heard a distant rumble of thunder. Soon the stars disappeared, covered with thick, black clouds. The rumbling kept getting louder and louder and you could see the streaks of lightning playing around the knife edge. The thunder kept getting louder, fairly making the basin ring.

One of the people says, "Hain't that terrific!" and another one says, "That sounds fine beside of that growling we've been hearing all day!"

Pretty quick, a big gust of wind came. I thought it was going to lift the camp right off its foundations. Then followed rain drops as big as teacups, mixed with hailstones the size of hens' eggs.

All night long it poured that way. The water was running six inches deep through the door yard. Then down the trail came the Growler, lookin like a drounded cat.

He says, "Could I come into the camp for a few minutes?"

I says, "Yes. Come right in and sit down and warm yourself."

He hadn't any more than sat down when he started chewing the rag again. "This is the worst sunken hole that I ever saw. A person ought to be prosecuted for coming into it!" he says. "Them fellers that's with me want to stay. They can stay if they want to, but I'm going out right now!"

I says, "You better wait. The rain might let up."

He says, "It can let up, for all I care. I'm going!"

I looked out of the door and snow flakes were falling as big as your hand.

He says, "How can I find my way down to Basin Pond?"

I told him to follow the telephone line.

So he put on his poncho. As his head come up through it I noticed his face was that narrow, he could drink out of a pig's track. He took off down the trail, growling and grumbling. When he was out of hearing the people all says, "What a relief to get rid of him! We'll take a little comfort, now."

By the time he got to Basin Pond the clouds had all lifted and the sun was coming up all warm and pleasant. Pamola stuck his head out of his cave and gave a shrill whistle. I waved back to him. The people all clim the mountain that day and enjoyed themselves. They put in a lovely day up there.

Well, I never saw the Growler no more. They say he didn't live a great while after he got home. I heard tell that after he died the doctor made an examination and found that he died of lint on the lungs. I think they said it was caused by chewing the rag.

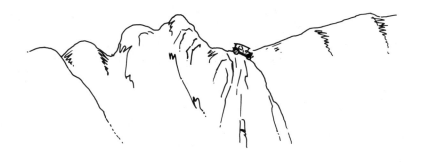

FROM THE PORCH STEPS
Clayton Hall

You are all asleep, quietly sunning yourselves. Dudley is back in his favorite rustic chair having a smoke. Far across the Great Basin comes the sound of Waterfall Gulley, a mile and a quarter away. Roy is scanning the great wall that brushes the clouds, the peaks carrying a touch of faded blue and purple in their deep folds.

The old man is getting impatient with all this quiet and turning his pipe about for a pointer, calls attention to a dark object on the Knife Edge. "See the Model T Ford!" he exclaims. We all look searchingly and discover the same to our satisfaction. Then begins a story:

Years ago a sculptor proposed to build a monument on the uppermost peak of Mr. Dudley's mountain. Henry Ford sent out Cragen, his Boston representative, to see about using their machinery to erect the monument. Mr. Cragen and the party arrived in a Model T. By superhuman effort they chugged up Pamola Peak, but crossing the Knife Edge was too much. "The rear end tore out." They abandoned car, machinery, monument and all. There it has rusted...ever since.

You could not find it possible to doubt Mr. Dudley, but the notion persists that what appeared to be a Model T is a peculiar stone formation — quite maddening to those who are sticklers for the truth.

There are several stories which are told from the cabin porch. A yarn told on the cabin steps is a legend embroidered on some natural feature of the Great Basin. Like a handful of semiprecious stones, the

55

rocks hereabout are never twice in the same light angle. They are constantly showing new facets, new faces. After long observation, there are to be seen in the steep ledge two vertical tracks cut in its weathered granite. These tracks are gauged perfectly as if cut for a mountain railroad. Here begins another story:

PAMOLA'S INVENTION

One bright moonlight night I heard an awful hammering and tinkering noise going on up at the peak. I couldn't see what was making it, but it kept on and on. So pretty soon my curiosity got too much for me and I headed up the Cathedrals to see what was going on. When I got near the summit I could see Pamola up there working away, busy as a bee, on some kind of contrivance. It seemed as though he was building something, but for the life of me I could't tell what it was.

Finally, he picked up some huge wheels to put on her and I could see she was a regular Roller-Coaster, to ride on down over the side of the mountain. Well, the wheels was made round on one side and square on the other, so they'd roll on the level places and slide on the steep places.

Pamola worked on it, there, for an hour or two and finally he got it all completed. Then he stood back and gazed his eyes over it and give a big smile. It suited him.

First he gave it a trial run down onto the table land. It went just as smooth as silk! It left a set of tracks, there in one place, part way to the Saddle Spring, then ran on by the spring a way and just stopped real easy where the land slopes up again to the north of the spring. That was great fun, so he dragged her back up to the summit for a real ride. This time he thought he'd go the other way.

So he sat down on the seat, gave her a little push with one foot and away they went. Well, things went pretty smooth from the summit to the South Peak and over the Knife Edge. Pamola was having a fine time! He whooped and hollered as he scooted

56

down the steep parts. The rig almost stopped, going over the humps. Then about Chimney Peak he ran into some kind of trouble. I was picking my way back down by that time so I wasn't looking at just what he was doing there. Next I knew I heard a yell. It looked like the roller coaster was running away! Pamola must have jammed on the brakes too hard and the wheels locked.

Anyway, there was an awful screeching and down he came over the rocks, headed straight for Chimney Pond! Down over the big ledge he came! The wheels were locked, cutting into the granite and sending slivers of rock flying all over the basin, right around my ears, too. But as luck would have it none hit me.

The roller coaster lit right at the bottom of the cliff by the end of Chimney Pond, and Pamola landed right in the pond! It must have made him awful mad, for he let out one blood-curdling yell, picked up a huge boulder that weighed somewhere in the neighborhood of four tons, smashed that thing all to pieces, picked up the chunks, and threw them way out in the middle of the pond. They're right in the bottom of Chimney Pond to this day.

On moonlight nights Pamola cuts up all his shindigs and antics. If you lie and watch for him you'll see him. Where Pamola put the brakes on is cut right into the granite rock. If anyone doubts this story, you can see the tracks right there on the face of the cliff.

THEM FLAT THINGS

Oft-times I go down to the shore of the pond and sit down and Pamola comes down and sits beside me. One night a few years back I was sitting there and Pamola, he came down. He seemed to be all talk that night. He told me, "This winter I want you to come to the mountain about the full of the moon in March. I saw some fellers last winter up here with some flat things on their feet and they seemed to be having great sport! Now, I'm going to get me a pair of them things, as near like 'em as I can, and I'm going to come down from the top of Pamola Peak on 'em. The ones those fellers had was about three inches wide and longer than they was, maybe seven feet long. What I'm going to do is, I'm going down to Millinocket and swipe a couple chunks of that boiler plate the Great Northern has piled up there, and make a pair of my own!"

So he talked on about how he would fix the bindings so's to hold them on his feet, and when we'd got it all talked over I come back to the camp and went to bed. The season passed by and time came for me to move out for the winter, but I left some blankets and food in the camp so as I'd have something when I came up to see Pamola do his skiing.

Come March, when the weather was good, two days before the moon fulled, I started on my snowshoes and come through the woods to Chimney Pond. I had no more than lit a fire in the camp when I heard Pamola's voice in the yard. He says, "Come out here. I have something to show ye!"

So I went out and there was his skis. I wish you could have seen them! They was twenty-five feet in length and about three foot wide. The ends of 'em was curled up like the nose of a toboggan, with a place for his feet, and the bindings was made of moosehide with the fur right on it!

He says, "How do them look to ye?"

I says, "Fine! Have you tried 'em yet?"

"No," he says, "I haint tried 'em yet. I'm waiting till the moon fulls. I'll let you know when I'm going to try 'em, so you can come out and witness some real sport. I think I can make as good a run down off the peak as I saw that feller make down Cathedral Rock last winter. If I can't do any better I'll break them flat things up and say I'm no good!"

The night the moon fulled, Pamola yelled at me from the top of Pamola Peak and said, "Come out!" So I went across the pond to the foot of the ledge. Pamola was lashing his skis on, tying knots around his legs with his raw moosehide.

Finally he said, "WATCH OUT! HERE I COME!" And how he did come on his skis, till about part way down, when he struck a patch of glare ice. Then one ski started up towards the South Peak and the other towards the North Peaks. Pamola tried to flap his wings to hold his balance, but he couldn't do it. Next thing I saw, he was all tangled up in skis and flying moosehide. Down he come, right towards me, sometimes head-first, sometimes feet-first. Sometimes he'd roll sideways, sometimes head over teakettle, and when he landed at the bottom he had jackknifed up and his skis had caught on the back of his horns. There he was, flopping his wings and going round and round sideways in a sitting position, same's a bird with a broken wing.

He says, "If I ever get these cussed-thundering things off, I'll never put 'em on again as long as my name's Pamola!"

I tried to get him to quiet down. I told him I'd try to get him free if he'd keep still. But he kept flopping and flouncing around so I didn't dare to get within fifty yards of him! At last he got exhausted. Then he says, in a feeble voice, "Come get me out of this, if you can. I'm about all in!"

So I went over to him, took out my hunting knife and commenced to slash up the moosehide bindings. Finally I got one ski loose. I tried to shift it back of his horns but it was so heavy I couldn't budge it. Then I worked and cut away the other one and Pamola straightened his legs with a sigh. Then he flopped his wings and shook them skis out from behind his horns.

60

He says, "What a relief!"

Then he straightened up, picked up the skis, and rolled 'em up as if they'd been paper. He says, "As soon as the ice is out, they'll follow that Roller-Coaster to the bottom of the pond! And the next time I see a party up here in the winter with them flat things on their feet, I'll send on blizzards so they can't get out of camp and try some trick and kill themselves."

Then he says, "I'll see you tomorrow night."

I says, "Aren't you going to try some trick down over the ledge?"

He says, "I've tried about all them tricks I'm going to!" So he bade me goodnight and flew over to his home.

The next night he came over. I met him down on the pond. He told me how lame and sore he was after the slide down over Pamola Peak. He says, "I suppose I'm going to keep on trying these fool stunts which I see people do, until I break my neck, which I very nearly done last night!"

I noticed he had his skis all rolled up under his arm. He says, "If I can make a hole through this ice, I'll sink these cussed things. So if you'll step off the pond..." So I stepped off.

Pamola flew way up in the air until he was very near out of sight. Then he folded his wings and down he come feet-foremost. He struck the ice with tremendous force and went slap through it in the deepest place where the water took him clean to his waist. Then he stepped out, picked up the skis, slipped them under the ice very easy and says, "Lie there, you cussed-thundering neck-breakers!"

THE FELLER CALLED EGYPT

I want to tell you about this feller we called Egypt. It seems as though it was the summer of 1930. Come the fourth of July, my wife and I decided we'd have a picnic to celebrate. We packed up our lunch the night before so we could get an early start and we set out before daylight for Sandy Stream Pond with our fishing gear. Well, we hit it just right and had us a good mess of trout by eleven o'clock. We cooked our trout right there for lunch. They never taste any better than the minute after they're caught. After we ate our lunch we headed back for Chimney Pond.

At Roaring Brook we could hear something coming along the old road from Windey Pitch so we waited to see what it was. Pretty soon we saw a man coming. From a distance he looked as though he was walking on all fours! He had a big pack on and a cane in each hand — all humped over like a hedgehog going to war! He looked as though he hadn't shaved in three weeks. He had a little black mustache, and bushy black hair, and he wore a funny little khaki-colored cap with a green celluloid visor. On his belt he carried a .22 pistol.

When he came up to us we spoke to him. He told us he was on his way to Chimney Pond for a couple of weeks. He seemed quite heavily loaded. He told us his name, but it was so strange we just couldn't seem to get it. Later on he told us he was born in Cairo, Egypt, so we just called him Egypt.

While we were talking, a party of college fellers came along and we all set off together. Egypt looked tired so I asked him if he didn't want me to take his pack for a ways, for I was going right to camp. "No," he says, "I can carry it. It only weighs forty-eight pounds."

So we walked along till we came to the old blacksmith shop and he sat down. He seemed to be all in so I said to him a second time, "You better let me take that pack."

"Well," he says, "you can if you're a mind to."

On top of his pack there was a gallon canteen and it was full of something, but since it was the Fourth of July I didn't like to ask what was in it. Every time I'd set the pack down or step over a hump, that canteen would say, "Goo-ud". One of the college fellers had his eye on it like I did and every time she said, "Goo-ud" his tongue would run out, but neither one of us said a word about it.

So I made the two thousand feet with the pack and waded about half the way. The first big rock we went over that canteen said "Goo-ud" and the college feller, his tongue ran out. I'd go over another rock and his tongue would run clean out around and lap his ear.

By the time we got to Chimney Pond and I set the pack down on the porch we all had our tongues hanging pretty well down the front of our shirts. We all were hoping for something tasty out of that canteen but we didn't say a word. Egypt, he came along, took the canteen off'n the pack and unscrewed the top. We all were standing there with our eyes laying clean out on our cheeks!

He says, "I won't need this any more!" and "Good-good-good-good-good!" it poured out — a gallon of water.

EGYPT IN CAMP

I guess you'd say Egypt was a rig. He wanted to learn to cook, you know, and camp. Wanted to learn everything about camping except cutting wood! He was with me two months and never cut a stove full.

The first thing I noticed queer about him was one day when he started to build a fire in the stove. He took off the lid, put kindling in, put some paper on top and lit it.

I says, "Your fire won't burn that way!"

He says, "It ought to. 'Good foundation under it."

Finally I showed him about building a fire in the stove. So he started in to fry a pancake. He got it done on one side. It's about half-an-inch thick. He tried to flop it over in the pan but it missed the pan and come down on the floor. Of course it lit raw side down so we scraped it up, threw it in the fire, and he started over.

This time I showed him how to turn it with the pancake turner. Well, he turned it the first time and he was so pleased he couldn't stop. He stood there and turned it and turned it till he had it worn right down no thicker than tissue paper.

Egypt was a great musician. He carried his flute and piccolo and when big parties of boys and girls would come in he'd march right up and down the trail with women and children and dogs following. You could hear the sweet melodious sounds over the waters of Chimney Pond and the South Basin, playing such tunes as "The Campbells are Coming," "Turkey in the Straw," and "The Drunken Sailor." He played the flute and piccolo, and he got so much wind out of it that when he'd go to blow the fire up, his cheeks would swell way out, he'd give one big puff and scatter the stove lids all over the camp.

EGYPT THE LOVER

One day a party of girls came in to camp and there was one amongst them— she was a real lively girl! So my wife and I got talking to her and we put her up to flirting with Egypt a little so we could have some fun. So she did and Egypt fell, a dead easy mark. He started for the wash basin with soap and towel, washed, shaved, combed his hair back, and tied the towel over it to make it lay. All this time the girl stood at his elbow skinning her teeth and rolling her eyes at him!

He got up to the mirror and tried to fix his little black mustache, but the best he could do, the corners kept drooping down. So he turned to the girl and said, "YOU JUST WAIT!" and he started for Millinocket, thirty-one mile, for some mustache-wax.

But the girl didn't wait! When Egypt got back she was gone. There was three days he never touched his flute nor piccolo; never played a tune!

PRUNE WHIP

One day Egypt was cooking and he says to me, "Did you ever make any prune whip?"

I says, "No, I never did."

"Well," he says, "I'm going to make some."

So he started to put his prunes to stew and when he read his recipe he found he had to have eggs. So he asked me if I'd lend him my packbasket.

I says, "It's none of my business, but I'd like to know where you're going, Egypt."

"I'm going to Millinocket to get some eggs to put in that prune whip."

He walked thirty-one miles, bought a half-a-dozen eggs packed in a box of wet sawdust that weighed ten pounds, came back to camp, and started in on his prune whip. When he got it done he give me a taste of it. It tasted to me like a mixture of glue and Meader's Salve,[10] so it set on the table for about a week. All at once it disappeared.

I says, "Egypt, what did you do with that prune whip?"

He says, "I ate it," but I never saw the dish it was in since. I think that prune whip is right down to the bottom of Chimney Pond today!

DIRT

Now there were two weeks that Egypt lived without using soap or water. He never put a bit of water near his face or hands the first two weeks he stayed with us; never washed at all. He was an awful sight, all grime, with a big hole torn in his pants. Finally I told him, I says, "Egypt, if you plan to stay here with us you've got to clean up." Some way that made him mad. He went around with his pistol, shooting up the sign boards till I got the gun away from him and hid it a while.

He just couldn't see what was bothering me and my wife. One day she was making biscuits. She'd rolled the dough out on the board when Egypt came along and stuck his dirty finger in it. She cut the piece off, and throwed it in the stove. He says,

---

10. Meader's Salve: A soothing ointment commonly sold door-to-door in the early 1900s.

"What'd you do that for?"

Then one day Abby, she was washing. She'd got the clothes all on the stove to boil. Egypt stood there and he saw them coming up to boil, so he thought he'd help out and punch 'em down. Instead of getting a clean stick to do it with, he picked up an old stick we'd been using to poke the fire with. It was all smut. Abby caught him at it and there was trouble in the family right off! Egypt went out to one of the leantos and sulked about an hour and then came in as good as could be.

I kept finding sand on the blankets in the bed where he slept. So I thought I'd watch him and I found out he never took his boots off when he went to bed. I told him he'd have to take them off, or he'd have to shift and sleep somewheres else. So after that he'd wait till everybody had gone to bed and he'd sleep under the table. He'd lie there all rolled up in his blanket like an Egyptian mummy.

THE TRIP TO RUSSELL POND[11]

Egypt had been with us about three weeks, now, and hadn't clim the mountain. So one day he told us he was going over to Russell Pond for a few days. He made up his pack, took his blanket and, as he had no hunting knife, I let him take mine and my belt ax. He bid us goodbye and said we'd see him in about a week, and away he went whilst my wife and I sat playing cribbage. He'd been gone about an hour and a half when the door came open with a bang and there stood Egypt in the middle of the floor. All he said about the trip was, "That's one hell of a note!" That's just what he said, and he'd tell me nothing about it at all! I think he must of went in a circle and thought it was another camp he was coming to.

---

11. Russell Pond is in the Wassataquoik Valley (pronounced "Wassatacook"), about ten miles from Chimney Pond by trail.

67

EGYPT'S APPETITE

Talk about a man eating! I never saw a man with such an appetite as he had! Boys, he only weighed about a hundred and twenty pounds but when he ate he'd swell right up just like a snake. People would look at him and say, "That feller'll die before morning!"

I says, "You don't know Egypt!"

He could eat as much at once as four ordinary men. For example, one night for his supper he put away seven potatoes, and a pound of corned beef, topped off with eleven pancakes and a pint cup full of prunes. Another time there was a party here with twelve boys. They'd cooked a six-quart pail full of rice, but they was afraid it was going to rain so they decided to go on down the trail right away. They told me, "Here's a kettle full of rice you can have." So I took it into camp.

Well Egypt was just starting to cook some rice so I says, "No need to cook. Here's rice all cooked!"

"Golly," he says, "don't you want it?"

I says, "No, I don't care much for it tonight. You can eat all of it you want."

So he started right in at it. He ate it pretty near all up for his supper and before he went to bed he cleaned it right out, every bit! That's straight!

PARTING

Egypt said he was to stay with us two weeks but it was two months and a half he stayed. You know he got so lazy I had to get a cat to put under his arm to breathe for him! Finally he bid us goodbye, took his pack and took the trail up over the mountain, headed back for New York. The last I heard of him was through a friend of mine in Boston who said he saw him heading South on an old bicycle.

So goodbye, Egypt. You know, every once in a while we strike some of the queerest jigs!

PAMOLA HAS A SMOKE

One spring, when the warm March suns came, the snow started to melt, and I commenced to think of Katahdin. I lifted my traps and I kept looking at the side of Pamola Peak. It seemed as though the snow would never leave it. Finally in May I looked out and the snow had gone, so I filled the old Willys Knight[12] full of gas, loaded my stuff in, stepped on the starter, and off she went with a CHUG, leaving a trail of blue smoke behind her.

When I got to Millinocket I bought a few things I needed and headed for Katahdin. For three days I was busy packing in blankets and food from where I'd left the car at Windey Pitch. Soon I got my camp in order and all my stuff toted up the trail.

Then along come one of them bright moonlight nights. I was at the camp all alone — nobody there — and kinda lonesome. I looked up towards the peak and I could see the silvery moon shining down on the waters of Chimney Pond. I filled my tobacco pouch full of the very best, took a good supply of matches, and started up the rocky trail. I reached Pamola Peak, and when I got there the moon was shining with bright light over towards Hamlin Peak and over on the big boulders which stood out like so many ghosts. As I stood there gazing I felt a gentle tap on my shoulder. I turned around and there stood Pamola!

"Friend," he says, "Did you come to visit me tonight?"

I says, "Yes, I have lots of things to talk over."

"Well," he says, "you be seated and we'll talk 'em over."

So I sat down alongside of Pamola and we started talking. Of course I have a habit of smoking. I took my pipe out and lit it, as I was sitting there, and I commenced to blow smoke rings. Pamola's eyes caught them, and he watched them.

He says, "Dear friend, you seem to get a lot of pleasure out of

---

12. The Willys Knight was an open touring car of about the same vintage as the Model "A" Ford.

your pipe. You know, I'd like to have a pipe so as I could make pretty rings, too.

"Well," I says, "Maybe I can make you one!"

He says, "I wish't you would!"

"Well," I says, "I've got to go out to town tomorrow for a few more things and I'll see what I can get you for a pipe."

"All right," he says, "you get the pipe and we'll have a real smoke."

So the next morning I started down to Windy Pitch and I went to town. I'd been thinking about what we'd need and I decided a beer barrel would be just right. So while I was picking up my regular supplies I started asking around about an empty beer barrel. It was the strangest thing! There wasn't an empty beer barrel in town! Every beer barrel in Millinocket was full!

Finally, I was talking to the blacksmith, and he remembered he had seen an empty tar barrel over back of the railroad yard. Well, I went and found it and I says, "That will have to do." Nobody wanted it so I took it along. Then I went over to the mill and got me a ten- foot length of three- inch pipe to make a stem. I went down to where they were building boom, and I bored a hole near the bottom of the barrel with a three- inch boom auger. I put the stem in and she made a perfect pipe.

Well, I loaded her on to the old Willys and went back to Windey Pitch. Lo and behold, there stood Pamola, waiting for me.

He says, "Did you get it?"

I says, "Yes, I've got it."

I took the barrel, screwed the pipe into it and held it up. Pamola took it and put the stem in his mouth. Then he took a mighty drag on it, heaved a big sigh, and said, "Hain't she a beaut!" He was so excited about it he wanted to carry me in to Chimney Pond, here, on his back so as he could hurry up and try it out. I don't suppose anybody had ever given him a present before in his whole life!

So I rode in to camp on Pamola's back that time. It was quite a ride! But when we got in here we realized we'd never thought a thing about tobacco! What in the world were we going to use to fill that great big pipe?

Well, we looked around. There were plenty of balsam boughs. Lots of little trees were growing to fill in where they'd all been cut off. And there was lots of birch bark. That burns good. And there was quite a bit of old tar paper where I'd been fixing up my roofs. So we gathered up a great big pile of balsam boughs and birch bark and tarred paper till we had enough to fill Pamola's pipe. Pamola says, "There," he says, "load her up and we'll show 'em where smoking first started from! So I jumped the balsam boughs into it and the birch bark and the tarred paper and I got it filled clean to the nozzle.

"All right," I says, "after supper we'll head on up for a smoke."

After supper I clim up to Pamola Peak, and the moon was just coming up as I got to the top. I hadn't been there a minute before up came Pamola with his pipe. Him and I sat down there on top of Pamola Peak and got ourselves good and comfortable. Pamola, he liked to dangle his feet down into the notch of the Chimney and I sat there on the ledge beside him. He set the pipe down between the two of us.

"Now," he says, "light it!" and I went to work and built him a little fire in the middle. Pamola commenced to draw on the stem and the fir boughs began to crackle. He blew out great rings of smoke as big as the great basin and he'd tip his head back and laugh to see the rings go. "Oh," he says, "what a comfort this is!" You could smell the sweet odor of tarred paper burning mingled with the scent of balsam boughs. "What a sweet flavor this tobacco has got!" he says. The aroma of balsam boughs and birch bark and tarred paper just permeated the night air. "It's delightful," he says. So the tar barrel commenced to get hot and the lovely essence of coal tar mingled with the others. It sent out a beautiful odor!

The smoke rings he made went rolling over and over, and the more he made the more he wanted to. Finally he got it smoked down handy to the bottom of the barrel and the tar barrel com-

menced to get hotter and hotter, he was pulling so hard at it. And down in there was a mean little piece of birch bark, no bigger'n your hand. Well, that caught ablaze and the next thing I saw was Pamola's head wrapped right in a ball of fire! He gave a whoop out of him and dove straight for Chimney Pond. Haley's comet had nothing on it! There was a trail of fire behind him over a hundred feet long. He went kaplunk into the pond.

I looked and the pipe lay there burning. I says, "What in the deuce made the fire? I don't see nothing. " I started on the clean run down the trail. I clim down just as fast as I could. I was some worried about old Pamola!

When I got to Chimney Pond, the water was boiling and bubbling, and I could see black junks of stuff that looked like sticks of pulp wood bobbing around in the water, but I couldn't see nothing of Pamola. The steam coming off the pond was kind of blinding me. I couldn't see much at all. After a while, though, the breeze came up and blew the steam away enough so as I could see around. There, sitting up on the first Cathedral was Pamola, and he looked sick, downhearted and forlorn. He looked so odd for a moment I couldn't understand what had happened, but at last I noticed that his whiskers was gone. Big tears were rolling down his cheeks.

I says, "Pamola, what's happened?"

He says, "You know what's happened! My pride and joy! My beautiful beard! All burnt to ashes!" I clim up to where he was sitting. He says, "CUSS on that old pipe!" His chin looked bare. The shorn stubs of whiskers were about four inches long.

"I valued my beard more than anything else in the world," Pamola says, "and look at it! It's gone! I'm ruined!"

"Now Pamola," I says, "your beard will grow out in a little while."

He says, "Well, it'll be months." Then I sat down beside of him, and I took my pipe out and lit it. He reached over, yanked it out of my mouth and ground it up in his hand. "Look out," he says, "you'll be burned up, too!" Away he went up to his cave and says, "I'm so ashamed of myself, I dassn't be seen. I'll go into my den and lie there till my beard grows out." So I went back to camp.

73

Early the next morning, before it was light, I heard voices and tramping of men out in the yard. Well, I got up and looked out. There was a big crew of men out there with two of the skinniest pack horses you ever saw. They looked like nothing more than two sacks full of ax handles. Man and beast, they were all loaded down with Indian pumps and axes and spades. I went to the door. The chief fire warden was there.

He says, "Where's the forest fire up here?"

I says, "Hain't no forest fire."

"Yes there is," he says, "we saw it, clean from town. It lit the whole village up and the watchman on Trout Mountain called it in."

Now I didn't want to tell about Pamola's pipe. So I says, "Oh, it must of been those darn boys! There was a party of young folks in here last night and they wanted to build a bonfire. I wouldn't let them build one here because the woods are so dry. I think they sneaked up on the tableland and had their fire there. That's probably what you saw."

"Well," he says, "you tell them not to do it again. We tramped about all night!" So I had them stop in for a cup of tea and they headed back down the trail.

Next morning I went down to the shore of the pond and the water was still hot. There was a row of burned whiskers all around the shore and I had to straddle them to get to the water. It was so hot and sooty, though, I couldn't drink it. I had to get my water from Cathedral Pool for about three weeks.

PAMOLA AND THE MOON

After Pamola's whiskers had been burned he lay in his cave in disgrace and sorrow. Every once in a while he'd stroke his beard.

"Oh," he says, "how long will it be before it gets grown out again? It's been hundreds of years growing and now do you suppose I've got to wait that long?" Then he'd stroke his chin again. "I think I can feel it growing now. If only I could go down to

74

Chimney Pond and look at my reflection in the water, I'd know if my beard is growing. Oh, I feel so ashamed of them shorn stubs all over my chin!"

Well I thought maybe he'd get better in a few days, but no, he just kept on mourning and sulking over the loss of his beard. He lay around for three weeks and hardly moved except to heave those big sorry sighs.

"It was my pride and comfort," he says. "It's gone. If it ever grows out I'll never smoke as long as I live! That was my first smoke and it'll be my last! What sense is there in smoking? It's a wonder a good many people don't get burnt up. I can see them going up the trail with pipes in their mouths and the smoke rolling out back of their ears. I wish I'd never seen a pipe nor ever heard of one. I'm fairly disgusted with myself to think of my whiskers nothing but burned stubs. Oh, oh, OH! That awful tobacco!"

I came to worrying about the state of Pamola's mind. It seemed as though he was really working at being miserable. Time passed on and he lay in his den, feeling sorry for himself for the better part of a month. Then came full moon time. I was sure I'd see him out that evening, but I clim up to his den just to be sure.

I says, "You know the moon fulls tonight."

He says, "SO WHAT?"

I says, "The moon's going to need you to help it across the Knife Edge."

"I DON'T CARE!"

I says, "What if it can't make it?"

He says, "I DON'T GIVE A HOOT! IT CAN DO WITHOUT ME!" So I figured that was that.

The moon rose, a great big silver disc, and it looked around for Pamola. He was nowhere to be seen, so it started to get across the Knife Edge by itself. It had some trouble here and there, but it rolled itself along pretty well till it came to that big hump up there just this way of the South Peak and there it hung — couldn't move another inch. I clim back up to the cave again.

I says, "Pamola, the moon's stuck on the South Peak."

He says, "TOO BAD!"

I says, "Aren't you going to do something?"

He says, "SHE CAN STAY RIGHT THERE AS FAR'S I'M CONCERNED!"

So she stayed right there for three days steady, shining all night and all day, right in one spot. Finally, Pamola looked out and he saw how the moon had been hanging there three whole days and nights, and he says, "I've got to get that moon across the Knife Edge, whiskers or no whiskers. Her mainspring must be stretched to the breaking point!"

So he crawled out of his cave and looked things over. The moon was right there, stuck tight on the South Peak, so Pamola goes over and he got behind the moon and gave her a push. She didn't budge. Then he got in under a bit and he lifted. She started to turn and he got her pretty near loose when she slid back on him. The spring was so tight and holding such pressure that Pamola couldn't get it over. Finally, he put his shoulder way under it, braced his feet with all his might, and gave one mighty HEAVE. With a terrible scraping the moon broke loose and went over the top of the Peak. Well you should have seen that moon travel! It went out of sight quicker'n any bullet you ever saw. In about half an hour it was rising again over in the East. It rose and set three times that night before it got back on schedule again.

Poor old Pamola went back to his den and lay down. He says, "I know I look terrible with these short stubs sticking out all over my chin like so many spikes. I hope the moon will be high next month so I won't have to get out where anybody can see me. I feel shamed and disgraced without that beautiful beard waving on my noble breast." So he still lay low for quite a spell.

77

PAMOLA HAS HIS BEARD TRIMMED

Well, Pamola was still lying around hiding from the world and waiting for his beard to grow back, when one day I ventured up to his den to pay him a visit.

"Can you see it growing any?" he says.

I says, "What?"

"My beard! With it looking the way it is now I'm ashamed and disgusted. It's a disgrace to be seen! I've put everything on it. I've even rubbed this oil on it. Hain't there some way to make it grow faster?

"Well," I says, "I can think of one thing that might work. Maybe I can help you."

He says, "I wish you would."

So the next day I went twenty miles right through the woods and I fetched in a fifty-pound bag of fertilizer. I carried it up to Pamola and I told him to rub it over his chin. Well, he did, and you'd ought to seen his beard grow! It just sprung right out! I heard Pamola laughing up to his cave. And I went up to see what he was laughing over.

"Oh," he says, "it's coming fine. It's going to be beautiful!" But he kept plastering the fertilizer to it and finally it grew so long it got down to his feet and it still kept on growing till one day he got out and whooped around and his feet tangled up in it and he took a header down over the mountain and very nearly broke his neck.

Then he came down to me and he says, "There's got to be something done. My beard is too long. I wish you would fix it for me."

I says, "You go over to that old fallen tree and kneel down and lay your beard right there across it." He did and I took my double-bitted axe and I stood there and I cut his beard just as straight across as I could. It looked just like a broom, the end of it, and I says, "Now go to the pond and see how it looks." He went down to the pond and stood on the rock and saw his reflection in the water. He says, "That's lovely! Oh, that's beautiful! This is the handsomest beard I ever saw. You're a barber as well as a doctor!"

I says, "Yes, I'm a jack of all trades."

"Well," he says, "you fixed me up in good shape this way. I'd just as soon be seen anywhere, now."

So I went out to cut some wood with my axe. You ought to have seen the nicks in it! Why it was just as though I'd chopped hay wire. The next day I had to get me a boy to help me for two hours to grind the nicks out of my axe before I could get a night's wood.

So the next day Pamola came down again to get his beard cut, it was still growing so fast. I says, "For the love of Pete, Pamola, wash your chin and get that fertilizer off! If you don't it'll keep me all the time cutting your whiskers and grinding the axe!" So I cut it off one more time, and Pamola flew over to Lake Cowles and took a good bath and washed his chin extra careful. After that his beard stayed in the good old shape, and Pamola felt happy and contented to fly around with it waving on his breast.

PAMOLA'S WHISKERS GO TO SEED

One summer on old Katahdin we had an awful cold season. It was so cold the snow never left the slopes. The ice never went out of the pond and there was snow everywhere through the woods that you could look. Poor old Pamola couldn't get no chance to take a bath. He lay around on the granite rocks and what few bare knolls there was. The wind blew the sand and soil and old dead leaves into his beard till they collected about six inches thick all over his chin, down in around the roots of his beard. It felt awful but he couldn't get a chance to wash it off.

So that next winter as he lay in his cave, this sand and soil, it fertilized his whiskers and they commenced to grow. Well they didn't grow quite as fast as when he'd put the fertilizer to them, but they grew DIFFERENT. They grew as much as three feet longer than they had been, and each whisker sprangled out at the end like a birch tree top. All winter Pamola lay there watching his beard growing and thinking how much more beautiful it was going to be.

So in the spring, when the warm June suns came, he was lying on the slopes gazing off, taking in the scenery and looking at the beautiful mountains in the distance. He lay there day after day with the warm June sun shining on his lovely flowing beard. Finally there was tiny little buds came all over it. At first he didn't pay much attention to them, but then they commenced to crack and Pamola's beard was covered with the prettiest little yellow flowers you ever saw. It was just lit'rally covered!

Well, Pamola was so proud of them he came and gazed in the clear crystal water and looked at his reflection in Chimney Pond.

"Oh," he says, "what a beautiful beard I've got!"

He would stroke it with pride. Then he would go up and lie with his chin over a rock and his beard hanging down so that all could see and admire the beauty of his whiskers and the reflection of them in the pond.

81

Well, after about two weeks the blossoms withered up and fell off, and on came tiny seed pods, such as you see on kale, turnip, mustard, and suchlike. At first they didn't bother Pamola. They was tiny, but they kept growing till they got to be about three inches long and the heft of them made poor old Pamola walk around stooped with his beard resting on his breast. It was such a heavy load on his chin he couldn't hold it up. Well, it passed on about fifteen days and they commenced to turn brown.

Finally they got ripe and some of 'em cracked open, and Pamola decided it was about threshing time. So over the mountain he flew, switching his beard this way and that way against the boulders, dropping a few seeds here and a few there till he got them all threshed out. It took the weight off his chin so he could stand erect once more.

Where every seed dropped there sprung up little tufts of wiry yellowish brown grass. It still grows all over the mountain and looks like hair. People see it and wonder what kind of grass that is. Some say it looks like Buffalo Grass and some call it Deer Hair.[13] But little do they know it's the seed of Pamola's beard and the right name is Pamola's Whiskers. You'll see it growing around the pond and on the plateau all in amongst the big boulders. And since that day till this, Pamola always keeps his chin clean.

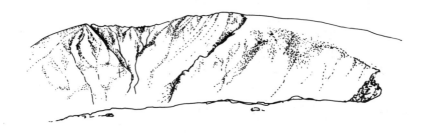

---

13. Pamola's Whiskers or Deer Hair: Scirpus cespitosus. See Appalachian Mountain Club, MOUNTAIN FLOWERS OF NEW ENGLAND, pp. 48-49.

PAMOLA HAS TROUBLE WITH HIS HEAD

One day Pamola come to me scratching the side of his head. He says, "Dear Friend, there seems to be something wrong with my ears. I'm afraid I'm going to lose my hearing for there's noises inside my head and I imagine I can feel something crawling around in there. I wish that you'd take a look and see if you can see anything.

I says, "Well, let me take a look in your ears, Pamola." So I got up and I took my flashlight and looked in Pamola's ears. Porcupine! Why, when I looked in there all I could see was white backs and quills going 'round! It was the worst looking sight I ever see! I says, "Now, Pamola, I can't kill them here on the game preserve. You'll have to fly across the line; then I'll take them critters out of your ears."

He says, "I wish you would."

So I went to work and made me up a hook. Then I got on Pamola's back and we flew down across the game preserve line. Well, I commenced to drag out porcupine and kill them and cut their feet off, and when I got through I had just a hundred and nine dollars and seventy-five cents worth of porcupine feet.[14] So you can judge what a mess it was in Pamola's ears!

You see, these porcupine had just denned up there. They live in under old logs and places like that. Of course they'd clim up on the side of the mountain, looking for a den. When they found Pamola's den and Pamola lying there taking his sleep, the porcupine thought his ears was a nice place to den up in. And sure they was. It was good and warm and comfortable in there, so they'd keep piling in till they got his ears filled up.

---

14. The State used to pay a bounty on porcupine; something like twenty-five cents for four feet. Usually the Town Clerks had the dubious privilege of receiving and counting the feet and paying out the bounty money.

Well, when I laid them out and Pamola saw them all stacked up, he says, "Did all them come out of my head?"

I says, "Every one of 'em!"

"Well," he says, "why couldn't you have took 'em out up there instead of coming down here?"

I says, "You know it's against the law to kill any wild animal on the game preserve. Wildlife is all protected, so I had to fetch you across the line, first."

"Well," he says, "you know, they're awful looking things!" He says, "When a man gets his head full of the like o' that, he can't think of much else, can he, nor hear much?"

I says, "No, he can't."

"Well," he says, "I'll have you clean my ears out every month after this."

I says, "Well, the State wants to get rid of them porcupine and they pay a bounty on 'em, so that's fine!"

After that, he told me his hearing was ever so much better than it had been. And I got along pretty well on the bounty out of porcupine.

That's how I come to pull through the depression, right out of Pamola's ears. They made a very good trap for me. Along with the other business it kept me going all the time. I would get about twenty-five dollars worth of porcupine feet out of Pamola, each cleaning. Of course they wa'nt as thick as the first time. They'd been collecting in there for years.

So the first time, when I took all them feet to the treasury, they was so many of them, why, the man looked at them and his eyes stuck out. He says, "Where did you get all them porcupine feet?"

"Oh," I says, "I hustled around and killed 'em under rocks and out of the trees." I didn't want to tell him I was using Pamola's head for a porcupine trap!

That's the straight facts about it.

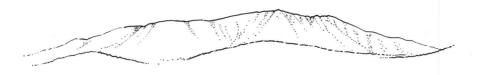

84

CHARLES IDOLPHUS

Late one afternoon I heard an awful yell down the trail. So I listened. "Just let me lay my hands on him ONCE!" Of course I didn't know what it was. I thought it might be some drunk or lunatic coming up the trail and paid very little attention to it.

I could hear somebody coming closer, though, still yelling now and again. Finally he rounded the bushes at the end of the trail. There stood before me the perfect specimen of manhood, six feet six in height. We'll commence at his feet and describe him up. His feet was as big as snowshoes. His arms was very long and hung down to his knees. Around his waist was two belts well filled with three rows of cartridges and on each hung a forty-five revolver of the old Beasley model. At one side was a long knife stuck into a sheath with the glittering handle sticking out from under his coat.

His hide was stretched so tight over his bones he couldn't close his eyes nights. His neck was long and craney. He had a thin, sharp, hooked nose and eyes like two peeled onions. They was so close together he had to wear interfering pads to keep one eyeball from chafing against the other. His jaw was undershot with two big teeth which stuck right up by his upper lip with points of both hid by a yellow curling mustache. 'Mind how those old Russian generals used to look, with mustaches like two horse's tails sticking out on each side? His eyebrows looked like two wisps of straw. His head was topped by a ten-gallon hat with a fifteen-inch rim. It made him look just like a toad under a cabbage leaf.

I gazed at him in amazement for a few minutes, and then he walked over to me and says, "Are you the ranger here?"

I says, "I am."

He says, "I'm Charles Idolphus Guildersleeves. There's a man here in the mountain that wronged my sister and left her in a most delicate condition. She had a child. The boy is the worst that I ever see! His mother is scared of him and I would be if I wa'nt an awful brave man. He has a little house built for himself out in the tree tops and it's marked all over with the skull and crossbones. No one dares to go near it. Why he's a regular little savage! I'll have his father go back there and claim his child or else there won't be enough left of him to swear by! Can you tell me where I can find the villain?"

Well, it was foggy in the basin, clouds in low, and it was getting towards dark, so I told him I'd show him in the morning where to find Pamola. Seemed as though that was who he was looking for all right.

He says, "That's all that's required. I'll make short work of him when I get my hands onto him."

I says, "He's a pretty hard man to do anything with."

"Well," he says, "I haint no spring duck myself. I'm just as loose as ashes and twice as dusty and feel just like a string of suckers! I was sired by a wildcat and suckled by a she-bear! My favorite drink is warm blood! I can smile at a dying man and his groans is sweet music in my ears."

I says, "Would you like to see Pamola's picture?"

He says, "Nothing would please me any better than to see the cold-hearted wretch!"

So I took out the picture that Mister Day took of Pamola and me, and showed it to him. He says, "Looks something like my grandfather, only Grandfather didn't have wings. I licked Grandfather once when he was ninety years old, too, and I gave him a good sound thrashing which he never forgot till the day he died." He says, "I'll show you how much a man amounts to in my hands. Where I come from we got into a scrap once and there were fifty men against me alone. I knocked 'em right and left and there were thirty-two of 'em would never fight no more. They dug the graves up on the hill back of my place and named the spot 'Idolphus' Burying Ground'."

So he talked on that way, told me of the things he'd done, the battles he'd been in and the men he'd killed. He said he had them all buried on this knoll back of his home. He said he could gaze for hours at it, looking at the grassy knoll and admiring his handi-work. It was three o'clock in the morning before he got all the gas off his stomach and went to sleep. Once he was asleep I thought that if he could fight as well as he could snore he was some scrap-per.

In the morning the clouds were all gone and it was a perfect summer day. I cooked breakfast and when 'twas ready I went over to where Idolphus was sleeping, give his foot a shake and says, "Come, Idolph. Breakfast's ready."

Well, he jumped and hollered, "MURDER! Take him away! He's killing me!" Then he rubbed his eyes, set up in bed, twisted his mustache three or four times and says, "I was dreaming that I'd killed Pamola. Turned Chimney Pond into nothing but a big pool of blood."

We had our breakfast: bacon, eggs, pancakes, syrup and cof-fee, and then Idolf took a string out and hung his guns down low; lashed the holsters down, strapped his knife on his forearm, curled his mustache in good shape and said, "Show me where the cold-hearted scoundrel lives!"

I pointed up to the big hole in the rocks. I says, "He lives right in that hole there, and if you want to find him you go right over there and you'll see a big stone hammer and they's a big thin slab of rock. You hit that rock and say, "Pamola, come out here! There's trouble waiting for you!"

He says, "I'd sooner fight him right here, where they's better footing." So he got out in the center of the yard and commenced to pound his breast and holler: "Come down here and fight! It's me, Roaring Charles Idolphus, brother of Sukey, the girl you wronged and left in a delicate condition!" Then he pounded his breast and twisted his mustache and the more he talked the braver he got. He says, "Come down here, you craggy-horned, picked-beaked, bat-winged, eagle-clawed, knock-kneed, batter-shinned, sickle-backed, gimlet-eyed son of a sea-cook! Stand up before a MAN, you woman-beater!"

But Pamola, he paid no attention. He was having his beauty sleep. Roaring Charles couldn't wake him with his roaring, but he says, "I'll fetch him!" and he reached for his big guns and commenced to blaze away at the mouth of the cave, fanning the hammers as fast as he could. Many's the time he emptied his guns that afternoon.

Finally a few bullets spattered into Pamola's den and woke him up. When I see Pamola's head peeking out of his cave, then I knew there was trouble coming. I says, "Idolph, you're in for it!"

"In for nothing!" he says, "I'll make short work of that hound!" There he stood, revolvers in hand, with his big yellow mustaches with curls like big rings on the ends.

Old Pamola slid out of his den ve-ry easy, and looked down at him. Idolph commenced to lace the lead at Pamola but the bullets just merely bounced off. All to once he put his guns up and he just stood there with his jaws open, kind of gasping. Pamola had come clear out on the rock, where Idolph could see the whole height and size of him, and just stood there with his arms folded, facing the north.

Next I noticed Pamola was kind of sucking his breath in. He begun to swell way up just like one of those hot air balloons till he was about two hundred feet around. Then he turned and blew south and went down to natural size again. He kept this up and just stood there with his arms folded, facing the north. I could feel the air getting colder and colder.

I says to Idolphus, "Why don't you try a shot at him?" But Idolph just stood there shivering, as pale as a ghost. The ends of his mustache was beginning to droop. He looked so kind of shaky that I took him up in the camp and made him sit down. When he'd sat a while I says, "Well, now, are you ready for another go at it?" Charles never moved except for trembling. There he sat with never a word, so I let him rest.

So night come on and Pamola still stood with his arms folded facing the north whilst Idolph sat there in the camp shivering.

Finally I says, "What's the trouble, Idolph?"

"Why," he says, "I haint feeling well."

"Well," I says, "run down and get me a pail of water."

So Idolph took the pail and went down. When Pamola saw him come out of the cabin he just breathed down on the pond. One breath froze the pond six inches. Idolph's pail was froze right into the water.

So he come running back and says, "I'm an awful sick man. I wish I was out of here!"

I says, "Where's that water?"

He says, "I couldn't lift the pail."

So I went down and I see what was up. There was six inches of ice on the pond. All of a sudden, the basin lit up light as day. I could hear a kind of sissssing noise, and I made up my mind that Pamola'd drawed in so much wind from the North Pole that he'd got a good share of the Northern Lights too. But I couldn't stop to watch the lights because I had to get back and tend to poor Idolphus.

When I got back, there sat Idolph by the stove, nothing but a suffering bunch of misery. His mustache he'd taken so much pride in was drooping by the corners of his mouth. His eyes rolled up so's all you could see was the whites. He was saying, "This is awful! This is awful!" over and over and trembling all over like a leaf. At last he says, "Haint there some way I can sneak out of this forbidden spot?"

I says, "Wait till daylight and then you can go, for Pamola'll be having a nap."

Idolph says, "I don't want to stop till morning. I want to go tonight!" He says, "It's good and light out there."

I told him that was just Pamola blowing the Northern Lights back into the Great Basin and outside he'd find it blacker'n the inside of a cow.

"I'm sick," he says, "and my nerves won't stand it till daylight."

Well finally I got him rolled up in a blanket. He took it and rolled it right over his head. Every once in a while he'd say, "Has he gone, yet?" All the time he's trembling and he kept that up all night long. I didn't sleep any either and I was glad when daylight come to get rid of him.

When it come good and light, Idolph got up and looked out. There stood Pamola in the same place where he'd stood the night before with his arms folded and facing the north!

Idolph fainted away three times. Each time he says, "I can't stand it! It's too much for my nerves!"

Finally, he says, "If you'll come down the trail with me I'll give you one of my six-guns!"

"Oh," I says, " I'll go down with you a ways." So we started on down the trail and he made me walk behind him. When we got to Basin Pond his legs stopped shivering, and he commenced to twist the corners of his mustache. When we reached Sandy Stream Pond he had his mustache pretty well curled up.

He says, "I fixed him, didn't I?"

I says, "Can you go out from here all right?"

"Oh yes," he says, "I can make her now," he says. "I'll need these six-guns going out, and I'll send one to you as soon's I get home." (But I never received the gun.)

So he pulled up a gun in each hand, held the knife in his teeth, and says, "If you ever want any hard battles fought, send for Idolphus Guildersleeves!" Then he bid me goodbye and started off on the clean run down the trail. I never seen him since.

So I started back for the camp. When I was getting quite handy so I could see, I noticed Pamola swaying back and forth like a huge tree being cut down by a lumberjack. All at once he tipped over. Down he come over the side of the mountain, bumpety bump, and landed in a bunch of white birch and scrub spruce.

The jar of it shook the ground and almost took me off my feet. It sounded worse than any landslide I ever heard. So I thought some of Idolph's bullets might have taken effect. I felt heartsick and sorry to think I had lost such a valuable friend.

I went right over to where he lay to take one last look at him,

90

and such a sight to behold! He was bloated up just like a small mountain by himself. But I could see he was still breathing. I says, "As long as there's life, there's hope!" I put my hand on him and he felt just like a big iceberg. "Now," I says, "I'll go back and see what I can do for him."

So I went back to camp, got my axe and saw and built a fire on each side of him. I kept cutting wood, piling it on, heating big rocks and laying them on his breast. All the time his breath kept coming out with that sisssssing noise. About the third day he opened his big loving eyes. He looked at me and says, "Doc," he says, "if you bring me out of this, I'll never do it again!"

So I het some big giant rocks, laid them on his breast and belly, and there was little brooks of water commenced to come streaming down over the side of the mountain. I knew that he was melting a junk of the North Pole that he'd drawn into his lungs. I could see him growing smaller all the time, getting down to his normal size. The next day he was on his feet.

I says, "How are you feeling, Pamola?"

"Oh," he says, "I'm feeling quite well, now. But I was so all-fired mad at that GOO-GOG making a racket and disturbing my slumber that I very near committed suicide!" Then he says, "Oh, if you'll just give me a hot drink like the time I et the moose!"

I says, "I will."

He says, "Make it good and strong!"

So I went to camp and fixed up a dose: two pails of water and four pounds of black pepper. Then I was afraid it wa'nt strong enough so I threw in a pound of red pepper. I give it to him and he drank the whole of it. He done it in two big gollops.

I says, "How's that?"

"Fine," he says, "and I feel a lot better, but I'm awful tired."

So away he goes up to his cave and he soon fell into a deep sleep and for two weeks we could hear his snores around Chimney Pond. They made a guggling noise like a whirlpool under a dam. Of course some of the mountain climbers was frightened when they'd hear it. I told them it was nothing to be afraid of. Pamola was only having his nap.

91

PAMOLA TELLS A STORY:
THE DUNGARVON WHOOPER

One spring night the moon was shining bright and everything was quiet around the cabin. Only now and then you'd hear somebody snoring so as to almost lift the roof off the camp. I looked out the window and the bright moon was shedding its rays on the waters of Chimney Pond. The mountain ash was all in bloom around the shore of the pond, the white blossoms showing in the moonlight.

I thought I wouldn't get a better night than this to see Pamola. So I slipped from the camp and clim up to our old meeting place. I'd hardly got seated when I heard a flopping of wings and there was Pamola coming over the Knife Edge!

I says, "Good evening, Pamola."

He says, "Good evening."

I asked him if he had time to tell me a story.

He says. "I have all kinds o'time." So down he sat beside me on the big rock and folded one of his big wings around my shoulder to keep the night air out.

Now I'll repeat the story, word for word, just as he told it to me.

"Well," he says, "this happened a long time ago, when I was a young man just at my full strength. It was one of the toughest battles that ever was fought. I didn't know for a while but what I'd lose possession of the mountain. For you know, if I lost possession of Katahdin I'd have to spend my time wandering over the country. I could be king of no big mountain.

"One night in August I was flying around over Katahdin, looking over my possessions. I stopped on the summit and stood taking in the scenery, feasting my eyes on the beauty of it and thinking, 'What a world this is to live in!'

"Well, I stood there gazing around and thinking how lucky I had been to be put in such a place, when all to once I was inter-

93

rupted with the most unearthliest yell that I ever heard in all my born days. It fairly riz the hair on my head. It shook the cones from the spruce trees, and I could feel the mountain tremble under my feet. It sounded right over towards the north.

"Then I saw a black object flying through the air. At first I took it to be a great black cloud, but as it drew nearer I could see it was a critter and had wings, same as I, and was sailing around over my mountain. I could feel my temper coming. I flew straight towards him and when I got handy enough I spoke and asked him what he was doing there.

"He says, `I'm going to make my home here on this mountain.'

"Well, I stood there for five minutes sizing him up without speaking a word. There he stood. He was bigger than I was, and he had a face that resembled an owl, with four big tusks running up each side of his beak. He had sharp sword-shaped horns on his head and a heavy mane like a lion. He had a long, smooth tail with a big hard ball on the end of it. His feet resembled the claws of an owl. He had the body of a man with wings like a bird.

"I says, `Who are you to come and take posession of my mountain?'

"He says, `I take what I please!'

"I says, `I was born here and this is mine! Fly back where you belong or I'll make trouble for ye!'

"He says, `What trouble could you make for me? I could spear you right through with these horns of mine. And that ain't all I could do!' Then he give that long tail a switch, fetched that big ball on the end against a granite rock and it slivered into a thousand pieces. I was getting real mad by then. I could feel my chin quivering and my whiskers bobbing up and down.

"He says, `I'll tell you what I'll do! I'll fight you for posession of this mountain. The one that wins'll have it and the other one'll fly away.'

"I says, `It's queer if I got to fight for my own holdings!'

"He says, `That shows the coward part of ye!' and that was the straw that broke the camel's back! I could stand no more of his insults and slurs. So at it we went! Such clawing and scratching you never saw! Sometimes we'd be handy to the edge of the basin, ready to fall down into the clearing. He would up-end, and that big tail would thrash on the ground, tearing up chunks a hundred foot square. Every time she'd strike, she'd send rocks and things flying down over the side of the mountain, leaving nothing behind at all.

"All night long we fought that way, striking and biting and picking and pulling one another's whiskers. When morning come he says, `Let's go rest till the moon comes up again.'

"I told him he could fight just as well in the day as I could in the dark.

"He says he couldn't for his big eyes bothered him.

"I says, `That's the darned owl in ye!'

"So I wanted to be fair. I went over and laid down, but I kept my eye on him so's he didn't do none of his treacherous tricks. If he could have crept up on me with that big tail of his, give me one swipe, he might have knocked out one of my eyes or broken a horn.

"Each night as soon as the moon was up, we was out and at it again and fit all night. "The blood was running down over the side of the mountain in streams. How them big sharp horns flashed in the moonlight! My greatest difficulty was to keep away from that tail and them swordlike horns. How the dirt and rocks splashed around my ears!

"So the seventh night we fit, I made up my mind one of us would be licked. We'd been fighting about two hours when I reached and grabbed one of them sharp horns. At the same time, I was driving my fist between his eyes with all my force. I could feel him tremble.

"Then I reached up my foot and drove my claws into his throat, all the time holding his head tilted back and putting these pile-driving blows right between his eyes. I could see him growing limp. Finally he gasped, `I will leave your mountain and never come back again.'

"So I let go of him and he fell over to the ground, nothing but

95

limp and almost lifeless. I stood over him and gazed down. I had sympathy for him. That big body lying there, trembling in the moonlight, shook the whole mountain so that one of the boulders rolled down off'n the slide. So I lay down where I could watch him.

"Along towards morning he commenced to show signs of life. Finally he stood up. I walked over to him and he says, `I'll never inhabit a mountain again!' So we shook hands and bid each other goodbye."

Over to Dungarvon Stream, lumberjacks sometimes hear him whooping. They can hear him as far away as fifty miles and he's knowed as the Dungarvon Whooper.

PAMOLA'S SON

Things went on pretty good at Chimney Pond, parties coming in and going out. They was cooking, chopping wood, climbing mountains, and so things kept on.

One time a party of students and professors come in and they stayed overnight. The next morning they started in and clim the mountain. Well, whilst they was gone on the mountain there was another party come in with a boy. Well this boy, he seemed to be interfering into everybody's business. No one could speak to him and get a civilized answer.

Late in the afternoon, almost dark, when the first party was coming down off the mountain, it started in to rain, so both parties come into the camp to cook supper, and this young one was right under everyone's feet and into everything. By the time they got their supper cooked we'd all seen quite a bit of him. He'd been getting in the way, butting in when folks was talking and telling them he knew better, till pretty soon no one knew what they was talking about.

Well, finally it was dark and still raining, so I says, "Now you won't need to go out tonight. We can make room for all of ye to sleep here all right." That was before we built most of the leantos.

One of the professors spoke right up. He says, "THE ONLY WAY I'LL STAY HERE TONIGHT IS IF YOU TAKE A ROCK AND TIE IT AROUND THAT BOY'S NECK AND THROW HIM INTO THE POND!" He says, " I WILL NOT STOP A NIGHT WITH THAT BOY IN THE CAMP, AND THAT'S FINAL! NOW YOU UNDERSTAND: I'LL WALK FROM HERE TO MILLINOCKET IN THE DARKEST NIGHT IN A DOWNPOUR OF RAIN BEFORE I'LL STOP IN THE CAMP WITH THAT LAD!

The boy kept right on, just the same. Finally I took notice of him, and I see on his head there was bunches coming out that looked like horns sprouting, and back of his shoulders was bunches coming on, right over his shoulder blades.

Well I talked to him some, and he says,"I come up here to find my Papa. My Papa lives here in this mountain."

Then all to once I remembered about Sukey Guildersleeves having a child. I knew then that this was the boy and Pamola was his dad. Them were the horns growing out of his head and the wings coming up on his shoulders. So I says, "Well, I'll show you where your papa lives."

He says, "I'll be very much pleased to find the place where he lives."

So I pointed out the way to the cave where Pamola lives and told him how to get there. "I'm going right up there now," he says, and off he started. Well, he clim up the side of the rock and he got about halfway up. Then some little rock slipped and rolled in under his feet and down he come, KA-THRASH, to the foot of the cliff. Then he come back to me and he says, "That old man lives in the cussedest place I ever see! I like to broke my neck!"

I says, "You wait till the moon fulls. It's just a few days, now. He'll come out and then you can have a talk with him." So about three days afterwards, when the moon fulled, he went up and sure enough, there was Pamola.

He went right over to Pamola and he says, "You know," he says, "that I am your son."

Pamola looked at him; eyed him all over from head to foot. "Yes," he says, "I think you are."

The boy says, "My marm's name is Sukey."

Pamola says, "She's the one that like to killed me! The worst woman that I ever saw! The only time in my life I ever got a real beating, she give it to me. Of course I'm man enough not to strike a woman, but we fit as thick and fast, there, as the Devil has the aching fever! Finally she left with a handful of my beautiful beard right in her hand and I was never so angry in all my days! I says, 'THAT AWFUL WOMAN! OH! OH! THAT AWFUL WOMAN! I SHALL NEVER GET MARRIED AGAIN AS LONG AS I LIVE!' But dear Son I am pleased to see you, my own flesh and blood! I can see my own features right in your face and even the wings that is sprouting out. Soon you shall have wings like your father and fly over the land. You shall view the whole country.

"Son, I'm awful glad that you've come and found me, for you can be a help to me in days to come. You know the ways of people and I don't. People have come and everything is changed. The mountain and the brooks are changed. When you become a man and have your wings and horns, you'll come back here and help me with the work there is to be done."

The boy says, "Well, Father, did Uncle Idolfus really give you an awful beating? He said he give you a thrashing you'd never forget, but I never believed him, 'cause I know he's the biggest coward that ever lived. Of course Mother upholds him. She thinks he's an awful brave man. It's 'Oh, Charles!' Everything's 'Charles, Charles, Charles! Charles this and Charles that!' I don't stand as much show around there as a dog. I have to get out and dig for myself the best as I can."

Pamola says, "Well, Son, in a couple years more I hope you can be with me. I'm awful glad to see you and proud of ye. You know, seeing you I can almost forgive your mother! I look at ye and see what a noble boy you are. When you come up to the cave I will show you the little carriage I made to wheel you in. It sits there with the wheels rotting down and rusting out. When you come up you can see it. Well, goodbye, Son. Good luck to ye."

So down come the boy and he told me, he says, "I'm awful glad I went up the mountain. I never knew I had such a noble papa. I'm proud of him. I want to be just like him. He tells me I'll have horns and wings and I'll look just like him in days to come, and I hope I do. Oh, what a beautiful beard he's got! Won't I be proud when I have them long whiskers lying on my breast when I fly around!

"So I'll come into the mountain every year, now. You'll see me here and you and I will be friends just the same as you and Father have been and I'll help you out. Well, I've got to go, now. The cars are leaving for Millinocket in a few minutes so I've got to get down there and get on home. So goodbye, and take care of yourself and I'll be seeing you again next year."

So away he went down the trail and of course that set me to thinking. I wanted to find out what the trouble was between Pamola and Sukey. So I made up my mind I would go up and see if I could find out what the trouble was; if Pamola would tell me how they made it with their courtship and how they lived together.

PAMOLA'S FAMILY TROUBLE

A few days after I seen that boy who was the son of Pamola and Sukey there came a bright moonlight night so I took my pipe and went on up the mountain to the place where Pamola and I liked to sit and talk. I just got set down there, on Pamola Peak, when I heard the sound of wings and Pamola lit on the boulder right next to me.

"Nice evening," he says.

"Yes," I says, "it's a beauty!"

He says, "I always like to sit up here with you, dear friend, and talk things over."

"Well," I says, "there's one thing I want to ask you, Pamola."

He says, "What is it?"

"Well," I says, "it's about Sukey. When you — when she — "

"What?"

"I don't know as I'd better ask."

"Oh yes — shoot ahead," he says, "I'll answer all your questions."

I says, "What was the trouble between you and Sukey that made you so angry, the time you threw the water out of Chimney Pond?"

"Oh, that FEMALE DREADNAUGHT!

"Well, my bowl was overflowing with happiness and I'd made up my mind I'd have a good happy life the rest of my days. So one night I went to the cave and I tried to make love to her. I put my arm around her but no, she wouldn't listen to it. It seemed's tho' she didn't want me in half-a-mile of her after I'd made all the calculations and preparations for a happy life! I thought, of course, of cuddling her, but Oh no! Just the minute I'd touch her she'd fly in a rage: 'KEEP AWAY FROM ME! Keep on your own side of the cave! There hain't room enough here for two!' My beard would switch over in her face and she'd get angry at that!

"'Get away from me,' she says, 'you old whiskered enemy! Get away from me! I don't want you anywheres near me!' My handsome beard flopped over and took her in the face and she grabbed right a-hold of it with both hands! I couldn't swing my head around quick enough. We fit all night long and when it was coming daylight, you believe me, I was some angry!

"She'd told me that first night that I was the lovingest and best man there was and she never thought she could find another one. For two days she was just as good as that, and then all to once she broke out in a sudden fury. Why, her face turned red and the spots shown out on it, and I thought she was going to scratch my eyes out! A wildcat's got nothing on her! I didn't want to hit her and I didn't, neither. I knew it wa'nt right for a man to hit a woman.

"So I held her away and the more I'd coax her the worse she'd act. She like to upset the whole place! Finally she says, 'I'm going out of this!' and she never stopped to slide down but she jumped right down over them ledges, ka-thrash! Then I got out on that rock, there, swung that big broom, and rolled that water around. I didn't do that, dear friend, to hurt you, but I was so all-fired mad at that daughter of Satan! I thought I'd show her what my wrath was like and give her a good washing to boot! That water struck in the trail right down on top of the hill and carried her pretty near to Basin Pond in the flood. That's the last I ever see of her and I don't know's I want to see her again.

"Of course I feel like forgiving her now, since I see the beautiful boy she presented me with. Why it's my own flesh and blood and likeness. You see it stamped all over him. Why he talks like me, if you notice it. And he has ways and actions just like mine!"

Pamola seemed to be thinking deeply. "You know," he says, "sometimes I think I would like to have her come back."

"Well," I says, "I might hunt ye up another woman."

"I wish't you would," he says, "I wish't you would — hunt me up another one. It's awful lonesome living alone here and I don't like to live this old life of a hermit."

PAMOLA'S LAST LADY-FRIEND

One late afternoon I was sitting on the porch here, looking up toward the mountain, and I heard somebody coming up the trail. I turned around and there come a woman, up here, a big woman, and she was walking just like a duck, great big flat feet, flapping along, and she came up.

"Hello," she says, "you got a nice mountain here."

I says, "Yes, it's a pretty good mountain."

"Well," she says, "I come up to climb it."

I says, "All right, come on up! We'll see if you can."

"Well," she says, "I don't know but what I will."

Well, I first looked her over. There she was, a great big wide flat face and a nose on her looked like a star-nosed mole. And she had great big ears that stood out and a big broad mouth that went clear from one side of her face to the other. Let a high wind come along and catch her with her mouth open, the whole top of her head would blow off! Well, her hair was bobbed and it was all frizzled up. It looked as though there hadn't been a comb in it for three weeks.

"I think you can cook your supper right over the stove here tonight. You can sleep in the camp if you want to," I said.

"Well," she says, "that'll be fine." And after she'd cooked her supper we set there talking, and she says, "You tell some stories, don't you?"

I says, "Once in a while."

"I wish you'd tell me one," she says. So I up and told her the story about Pamola. She says, "Is he here in the mountain now?"

I says, "Yes, he's right here now."

She says, "When could anyone see him?"

I says, "You can see him tonight if you want to. It's a moonlight night."

"Why," she says, "could you go up with me so I could see him?"

I said, "Sure, I would. What you want to meet him for?"

"Well," she says, "I want a man." She says, "I want a man. I'd marry any man," she says, "that wears pants."

I says, "Well, Pamola don't wear pants."

"Oh, well," she says, "that makes no difference. I'd marry him just the same."

"Well, then," I says, "I'll go up with you." But I didn't think she could see to walk, her eyes were so crossed. One of 'em looked down here, the other one up in the sky. But finally her and I started and went on up. Well, I got to the old rapping place and I gave the signal and up came Pamola.

"Well, Pamola," I said, "I thought I'd come up and see you."

"Yes," he said, "you picked another girl for me. I hope she proves better than Sukey!"

"Yes," I says, "here she is."

He says, "What's her name?"

I says, "It's Arvesta Pelateekahawn." I says. "Miss Pelateekahawn, meet Mr. Pamola."

So they shook hands, sat down and commenced to talk. "Well," I says, "I'll leave you people alone and go down."

So Pamola, he was looking down at her. "Oh," he says, "what beautiful eyes you've got!" He says, "What a lovely face!" He says, "I think you're the flower of the country and I'm awfully glad you came to see me." And he put his arm around her and hugged her up to him and I heard something that sounded like a horse's foot being pulled out of the mud. I think Pamola kissed her.

"Oh," she says, "you're a darling man," she says. "How did I ever happen to find such a gorgeous man as you are?"

Pamola says, "Get on my back now, and I'll carry you over the mountain and show you what I've got, here. Let me show you it all tonight." So she clim on his back and away they went over the mountain, and I returned down to the camp.

The next morning she came down and she was all smiles! "Oh," she says, "what a darling man that is! How can such a

104

lovely man live up in this mountain? And how I do love these big strong men the same as he is! He's just the right kind of a man for me. Just what I wanted! I couldn't have picked one or had one made any better than what he is. I just know my family will love him as much as I do!"

I says, "You plan to take him home to meet the family?"

"Oh, yes," she says, "I can hardly wait!"

I says, "You got a big family?"

She says, "There's just the six of us girls. Mother and Father have passed on."

I says, "What a shame."

"Oh," she says, "it's all right. The house was pretty crowded before."

I says, "Don't you miss them?"

Just then I noticed a shadow pass over the trees outside and I knew Pamola had lit out beside the camp. He couldn't help hearing when she said, "We don't miss them a bit. They was just a nuisance to us and the boys."

"Boys?" I says.

"Oh, yes," she says, "we had four brothers, but they're all gone, too. They all sort of wore out from tending the pigs."

I says, "Wore out?"

"Well," she says, "you can't expect ladies to do the farming! We're all too busy with our hobbies and clubs. Oh, I just can't wait till Mr. Pamola meets my sisters and our girl friends in the garden club. They'll just adore him! I just know it! Oh, Oh! I can't wait!"

I could see the bushes trembling outside the camp window, so I knew old Pamola was getting himself an earful.

I says, "So what do you plan to do next?"

"Why," she says, "I TOLD YOU. I'M GOING TO TAKE HIM HOME WITH ME. A LOVELY MAN LIKE THAT CAN'T GO ON LIVING IN THIS OLD MOUNTAIN. BESIDES, WE NEED A MAN TO DO THE FARM WORK, AND...."

Just then we heard the awfulest shriek I ever heard in my

whole life. Worse than the Dungarvon Whooper and louder than six steam whistles with a herd of wild elephants thrown in for good measure. Rocks and tools and firewood flew all over the clearing as Pamola flopped those big wings of his in his haste to take off before it was too late. My grindstone broke loose and went rolling off into the woods so's I was three days finding it. Such is the power of a desperate man!

Inside of half a minute Old Pamola was a wee speck far off in the distance out over the Wassatacook Valley. I don't know where he went, but it was three weeks before I seen him again. By that time poor Arvesta had given up and gone back home in tears, without her man.

Finally, late one night, just before the full moon, I was sitting in the camp here, reading some magazines one of the people had left behind. I was right in the midst of a good old tear-jerker of a dog story when I come to have a FEELING. I hadn't heard a sound, but I just KNEW that Pamola had lit right outside the camp. I picked up my flashlight and went out on the porch.

The moonlight was lovely, turning the Cathedrals all to silver, while Pamola Peak was one solid black shadow, but I couldn't see a sign of Pamola. Still I knew he was out there. I had a FEELING.

So I was standing there, admiring the beauty all around me and wondering where Pamola was when I heard a "PSST!" There he was, hiding behind the corner of the camp. "Is she gone?" he says.

I says, "Yes, she's gone."

"Are your sure?" he says, "Are you ABSOLUTELY POSI-TIVE?"

"Yes," I says, "I'm absolutely positive. She left twelve days ago."

Old Pamola shivered. "So she's had time to come back. I'd better get out of here." Poor Pamola looked all played out. He was thin and haggard and had a hunted look. It like to broke my heart to see him suffering so.

"No, no," I says, "she ain't never coming back here. She took a solemn vow. I think she means to give up men for life. I think

106

you broke her poor heart forever."

"Broke HER heart!" he says, "BROKE HER HEART! HOW DO YOU THINK I FELT?! Poor heart, indeed! Katahdin itself is soft-hearted compared to that scheming female! WHOOH! What a close call! WHAT A CLOSE CALL! I DON'T KNOW ABOUT HER, OR CARE, BUT I'M SWEARING OFF WOMEN FOREVER!"

I says, "I'm sorry you were disappointed."

"'Twan't your fault," he says, "HOW CAN ANY MAN KNOW WHAT TO EXPECT OF A WOMAN ANYWAYS?!"

PAMOLA'S BIRTHDAY

Pamola and I, we got pretty well acquainted after all our adventures. I remember one night when we got real chummy. It was moonlight and there was no one at the cabin. Pamola came down and asked me to go on a moonlight excursion with him, so I told him I would.

"Well," he says, "you come with me." So he got himself down and he says, "Now, climb right between my horns and get a good hold! I can fly with you all right from there."

I says, "Won't I be awful heavy on your neck, Pamola?"

"Oh," he says, "you don't amount to nothing!"

So I got on and got my hands hitched in the hair in his head in good shape. His hair was kinda hard to sit on, being coarse and stubbly, but I says, "All right, let her go!" His wings give a flop and up in the air he goes and over the mountain.

Such a beautiful sight I never thought of seeing on Katahdin! The moon was bright as day and I set and watched the beautiful shadow of Pamola's big wings as he carried me along. Away he riz in the air, over hill and dale, across the Klondike, and from one mountain peak to another. We cruised over The Owl, over Barren, over O.J.I., up over Coe, over The Brothers and over Fort. Then we circled back into the Northwest Basin, and up over the Northwest Plateau. I kept watching the shadow of his wings upon the green trees and scrub below us. In the moonlight night I could see clouds and ponds with clear water shining in the distance. I hung on like an old witch gripping a broomstick.

Away we went! The wind was blowing hard against me and Pamola was making a fast trip. As we put over the Northwest Plateau, he says, "You see this is awful level and smooth. Here's where I fought the Dungarvon Whooper, one of the toughest battles I've ever fought in my life. That's why the ground is trodden so smooth and hard."

When we got to Pamola Peak, we lit. I got down on the rock.

He says, "Don't you think this peak is more beautiful than all the rest?"

I says, "I do."

He patted me on the back and says, "Bless you, Bub! I like it myself. It's my home and it always has been. One time it was the highest peak on the mountain. What prettier scenery could you get than looking down over that slope and seeing all them pretty flowers in bloom amongst them granite rocks!" He looked at it for a good five minutes and kept saying, "How beautiful! How beautiful it is!"

And it really was beautiful to see the flowers and the mountain peaks looming up like so many sentries standing on guard, with the silver of lakes as far as your eye could extend. It's a night I shall never forget. It was one of the most beautiful sights that I ever saw in my days. And I was like Pamola. I says, "Beautiful!"

Whilst we set there I says, "Pamola, we've been friends for a long time. But the days are not far off when you and I part. I would like for you to tell me where you came from and who your folks was."

Pamola, he patted the big boulder he was sitting on. "This mountain is my mother. I was born from the rocks right on this slope. I will tell you back as far as I can remember.

"It was a long, long time ago, when Pamola was the highest peak on the mountain, hundreds of feet higher than what 'tis now. I was living, in them days, in a big boulder, kind of egg-shaped, that laid right on the very peak of the mountain. So the years passed by and the rock began to crumble and waste away, and the gravel gave 'way under my boulder, which I was in. Down it went, crashing over the side. I could feel it bouncing and going.

"Finally there was a heavy crash. I lay there unconscious for a long time. When I come to, I looked and see my shell was broken. That was the first glimpse of daylight I ever saw. Everything looked so beautiful to me! I stared until the tears rolled down my cheeks like raindrops.

110

"I had some difficulty in walking at first. I would stagger and sometimes fall down. Finally I got so I could walk pretty good, but these big wings hung down by my sides, useless. I couldn't flop them and fly the way I do now. But after about a year I got so I could move them and in a little while I could spread them out. Many a night I'd climb to the top and spread my wings and glide down into Chimney Pond.

"I'd strike about where your cabin sits and then I'd have to walk clean back to the peak and try it over again. Every time I was improving, getting so I could flop them a little more, and my wings getting stronger and bigger. At last I got confidence enough in myself so I could rise up in the air and sail around over the top of the lovely mountain. That is about all I can tell you about myself."

I says, "Pamola, that is very interesting. Now I must bid you good night and go to the cabin and get a little rest."

He says, "Dear friend, I will carry you down to your cabin to save you that walk. I have all day to sleep, tomorrow."

So I got onto his back. In one minute he landed me on the porch of Chimney Pond Camp.

"Good night, Pamola."

"Good night, Friend."

THINGS TO READ ABOUT KATAHDIN:

Clark, Stephen, KATAHDIN, A GUIDE TO BAXTER STATE PARK AND KATAHDIN, Thorndike Press, Thorndike, Maine. Good general information and history about Katahdin and the Baxter Park area. Includes map.

Leavitt, H. Walter, KATAHDIN SKYLINES, Maine Technology Experiment Station Paper No. 40, Orono, Maine; University of Maine Press, 1942. Reprinted by Thorndike Press, Thorndike, Maine. Somewhat outdated now and pretty much replaced by Steve Clark's book, but still interesting reading.

Appalachian Mountain Club, THE A.M.C. MAINE MOUNTAIN GUIDE. A guide to trails in the mountains of Maine. The Appalachian Mountain Club, Boston, Mass. Revised frequently. Informative for the hiker. Includes maps.

DeLorme Publishing, DELORME'S MAP AND GUIDE OF BAXTER STATE PARK AND KATAHDIN, DeLorme Publishing Co., Freeport, Maine.

Hakola, John W., LEGACY OF A LIFETIME, TBW Books, 1981; distributed by the Baxter State Park Authority. Complete and authoritative history of Baxter's acquisition and development of the area around Katahdin as a state park.

Baxter State Park Authority, A GUIDE TO BAXTER STATE PARK AND MOUNT KATAHDIN IN MAINE, Baxter State Park Authority, 1981. General information and description of the park and Katahdin; written especially as a guide for first-time park visitors.

Caldwell, Dabney W., THE GEOLOGY OF BAXTER STATE PARK AND MOUNT KATAHDIN, Maine Geological Survey, Department of Forestry, Augusta Maine. 1972. Interesting and readable.

Baxter, Percival Procter, Constance Baxter, Judith A. Hakola and John W. Hakola, GREATEST MOUNTAIN: KATAHDIN'S WILDERNESS, Scrimshaw Press, 1972. This is a fine "appreciation-type" book, with interesting descriptions and history as well as lovely photos accompanied by appropriate and sometimes poetic quotes from the late Governor Baxter.

ON FOLKLORE

Beck, Horace P., THE FOLKLORE OF MAINE, Lippincott, Philadelphia & New York, 1957. A delightful book to give one a perspective on Maine's story-tellers and songsters.

Beck, Horace P., GLUSKAP THE LIAR AND OTHER INDIAN TALES, Bond Wheelwright, Freeport, Maine, 1966. If all the Indian tales you've heard were in children's versions, here's a chance to get your teeth into something meatier. Maine and the Maritimes, mostly; good reading.

Eckstorm, Fannie Hardy, THE KATAHDIN LEGENDS, reprinted from APPALACHIA, Appalachian Mountain Club, December, 1924. Available in many libraries. Eckstorm recounts the main documented Indian tales about Katahdin, including the basic Pamola story. This is where Dudley took off from.

Eckstorm, Fannie Hardy, OLD JOHN NEPTUNE AND OTHER MAINE INDIAN SHAMANS, 1945, A Marsh Island Reprint, Orono, Maine, 1980. More background behind Neptune, who was the original source for the Dudley family. Interesting.

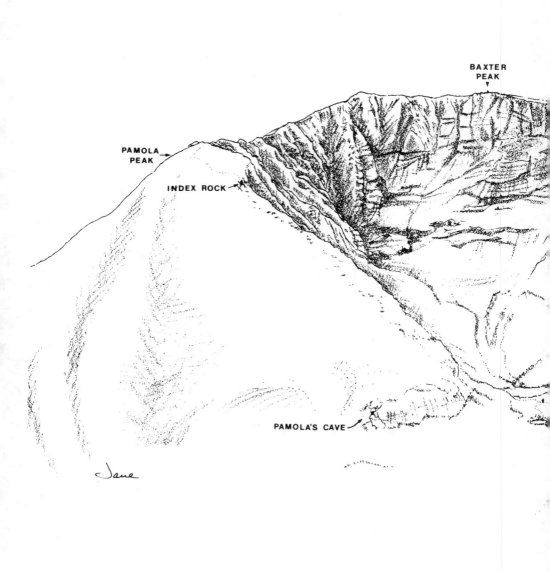

BAXTER
PEAK

PAMOLA
PEAK

INDEX ROCK

PAMOLA'S CAVE

Jane

CHIMNEY
POND

Pamola's World